RANGER LOYALTY

TEXAS RANGER HEROES

LYNN SHANNON

Ask, and it shall be given you; seek, and ye shall find; knock, and it shall be opened unto you.

Matthew 7:7

ONE

The window rattled.

Olivia Leighton jumped, glancing over her shoulder at the dark alley beyond the windowpane. The motion detection light on the side of the building clicked on.

As if someone was moving out there.

Fear crimped her insides. She rose from her desk chair, her heels silent on the plush carpeting as she drew closer to the window. Weak yellow lighting spilled from overhead. It illuminated the pavement directly outside, but cast long shadows near the dumpster. Shadows big enough to hide a person in.

Was her stalker out there? Watching her?

She'd been receiving notes for weeks. When the first one appeared in her mailbox, she'd thought it was some kind of sick joke. But then another was slipped under the door of her office. A third tucked under the windshield wiper of her car while she was running errands in town.

Olivia had reported them to law enforcement and Police Chief Sims had taken it seriously, but without knowing her stalker's identity, nothing could be done.

She'd installed a new security system for her home and office. Slept with a knife in her nightstand. Changed her routine. She was doing everything possible to protect herself, but the constant stress was wreaking havoc on her mental state.

I'm watching. I'm waiting. Soon it will be time for us to be together forever.

Those parting words in the stalker's last letter haunted Olivia. A shiver raced down her spine as she peered into the alley. Her heart thumped in an irregular beat, blood rushing through her veins, filling her ears with the noise.

Suddenly, a shape flew out of the darkness.

Olivia yelped. She jerked away from the window as the creature flew down the alley. Dark fur and black eyes.

A raccoon.

She pressed a hand to her racing heart as the animal ran through the beam of light before scrambling under a broken fence board into the neighbor's property. Olivia sagged against the wall in relief. She closed her eyes. Then sucked in a deep breath and mentally berated herself for freaking out. She was losing it. Yes, her stalker had sent letters, but to her knowledge, he hadn't done anything more than that. She couldn't keep jumping at every shadow.

Olivia snapped her eyes open. Her office was bathed

in warm light. Mood boards for a string of weddings coming up this spring and summer lined the far wall. For the first time since opening Blessed Events, Olivia was fully booked. It'd taken three years of hard work to get her event-planning business off the ground. In the beginning, she'd done birthday parties and corporate dinners. Her passion was always weddings though. One or two clients gave her a chance for a deep discount. Word spread. She was now the most sought after wedding planner in the Texas Hill Country.

It was a dream come true. But it would all fall apart if she didn't get it together. A wedding planner's job was to remain calm during chaos. Be a problem solver. She couldn't accomplish any of that if fear and anxiety crippled her. Enough was enough.

Olivia snapped the blinds shut on the window, symbolically closing off her concerns about her stalker. The police were looking for him. And God was protecting her. She would continue to use caution, but fear would not run her life.

A loud chime came from her desk. Olivia hurried across the room. She searched for her cell phone among the seating table charts and wedding cake photos, finally unearthing it from under a pile of catering menus. "Blessed Events, this is Olivia."

"Hi, Olivia." A deep voice with a slight Texas twinge rumbled from the speaker. "It's Cole."

Texas Ranger Cole Donnelly. Olivia's heart skipped a beat, this time for an entirely different reason, as an image of the last time they'd seen each other formed in her mind. At a tux fitting. Cole was strikingly handsome on a good day, but in formal wear... he was stunning. His chiseled jaw was clean-shaven, leaving all the focus on his arresting mouth and strong cheekbones. Tousled dark hair curled at the collar, adding a charming and almost boyish touch to his otherwise purely masculine features. If his face didn't make every single woman in visible range screech to a stop, then the rest of him did. Muscles were visible even though the thick fabric of his jacket and slacks hugged slender hips that gave way to powerful thighs.

Cole was a groomsman for a wedding she was in the process of planning for Elijah Goodwin and Sienna Evans. He was also the reason Olivia was still in the office at eight o'clock on a Tuesday night. She was waiting for him so they could discuss his speech for the wedding. Something Cole was incredibly nervous about.

She hoped he wasn't calling to cancel. The wedding was in a couple of weeks and Cole's schedule was hectic due to his job.

"I'm running late." Cole sounded stressed, a note of exhaustion peppering his tone. "It was unavoidable, and I'm sorry, but I'm on my way. Can you wait? I should be there in about fifteen minutes. If I don't speed."

"Don't get pulled over by the Serenity Police Department. They take speeding in town seriously, and as an outsider, you'll be given a lecture on top of it."

He chuckled. "A well deserved one too. Okay, I won't speed." He paused for a moment. "Have you eaten dinner? Cuz I haven't and I'm starving. There's an Italian place on the outskirts of town I've heard is very good."

She knew exactly which one he was talking about. "Romeo's."

"That's it. If we meet there, it'll shave five minutes off my drive time. My treat. What do you say?"

For half a moment, Olivia wondered if this was Cole's way of asking her out on a date. A riot of butterflies fluttered in her stomach. It caught her off-guard with its intensity. They'd seen each other several times in the last year and there was definitely a spark between them. One Olivia wasn't sure she wanted to pursue. Since losing her fiancé three years ago, she'd put romance on the back burner.

She needed to keep things professional. Olivia busied her hands by clearing her desk. "Dinner would be great. But I'll pay. It's a business meeting after all."

"No, ma'am." Cole's tone brooked no argument. "My grandmother would box my ears if I let a lady pay for her meal. Besides, I'm the one running late. And I'm pretty sure helping a groomsman with his speech isn't one of your duties as a wedding planner."

He was right. It wasn't part of her normal duties, but Olivia always went the extra mile for her clients. "I don't mind."

"And I don't mind paying for dinner. See you there."

Olivia hung up, a smile on her lips. She spent the next ten minutes running through tomorrow's schedule, and then hurried through her nighttime ritual of locking up. Cool night air stroked her cheeks as she stepped onto the sidewalk. The end of February carried a nip in the air, but in a few weeks, the nights would be warm enough for outdoor receptions. One of the benefits of living in Texas. Spring and fall were mild with glorious sunshine and riots of flowers. They paid for it in the summer—June through September was brutally hot—but Olivia always considered the trade-off worth it.

She hummed a tune while locking the front door to her small shop on the corner of Main Street and Elm. At this time of night, Serenity was quiet. Most of the residents were nestled snug at home.

Olivia hiked up her laptop bag on her shoulder. Then groaned. Her car was parked on the other side of the playground. There hadn't been any spots available near her office, thanks to today's craft fair. Visitors from adjacent towns ate from food trucks, bought handcrafted items, and let their kids play in the inflatables near the park.

It wasn't a long walk, but the dark shadows lingering beyond the cheery glow of the streetlights made Olivia nervous. She moved to the center of the road. Stoplights flashed yellow, warning drivers to be cautious, but at this hour, the streets were empty. Her heels tapped against the asphalt. Another gust of wind fluttered the strands of her hair and iced the tops of her ears. She pulled the collar of her jacket up to ward off a chill.

Footsteps echoed behind her.

Olivia's heart jumped in her throat and she glanced over her shoulder. No one was there. Still, the feeling of being watched caused goosebumps to rise on her arms.

Real or imaginary, Olivia couldn't tell. She'd jumped at a raccoon earlier tonight. Her instincts weren't finely tuned. Still, she slipped a key between her fingers as a makeshift weapon and picked up her pace as the park came into view. Her car was just on the other side.

The swings rocked on the playground as if pushed by invisible hands. It added to the intensifying fear knotting her insides. Darkness embraced her as she stepped onto the path cutting across the park.

Footsteps came from behind her once more. Olivia dared a peek over her shoulder. Her pulse skyrocketed.

Standing in the street, under the bright lights, was a man. His face was shrouded, hidden by the hoodie pulled over his head.

Her stalker? No, it couldn't be. Her mind rejected it, even as horror sank into her with icy claws. Olivia broke into a run. Her laptop bag bounced against her hip. The thunderous sound of her own racing pulse blocked out everything else, but she could feel him. Closing in. Her SUV came into view and she dared another peek over her shoulder. He was in the park. Less than a dozen yards away.

She tripped. Olivia's hands immediately shot out to break her fall. The keys in her left hand jabbed the delicate skin of her palm as they collided with the ground. The laptop bag slid from her shoulder into the grass. Hysteria sent her scrambling to her feet. She left her computer where it was. Getting away was all that mattered. Her breath came in rapid gulps as her anxiety heightened. She was going to have a panic attack.

"Sweetheart, don't run."

His voice came from right behind her. It was smooth and haunting, with just the barest hint of a Southern accent. Bile rose in her throat. Her fingers shook so hard Olivia couldn't hit the button to unlock her vehicle. The headlights flashed as the car finally responded to her desperate demand. She flung the driver's side door open and clambered inside, slamming the locks closed again immediately. Her gaze shot to the park beyond the windshield.

He was there. Still standing in the shadows.

Olivia struggled to shove the keys in the ignition. Sweat gathered on her brow and her heart beat like a drum against her ribcage. She couldn't breathe. The terror and panic were all-consuming. Almost debilitating.

The key finally slipped into the ignition and Olivia twisted it to start the engine.

Nothing happened.

"No!" Shock stole the last of her breath. She tried to start the car again, but the engine didn't make a sound. Olivia glanced out the windshield. The shadowy figure was closing in. Fresh anxiety coursed through her as a horrifying thought burst into her mind. Maybe he'd done this to her car. Disabled it so she couldn't get away.

Olivia yanked her cell phone from her pocket intending to call the police, but in her panic, dialed the last person who'd called her. Cole answered on the first ring.

"He's after me." The words spilled from her mouth in a frantic rush. "I can't start my car and he's here—"

"Who?"

"A man." Tears pricked her eyes. He'd come for her. Just as he promised. "Someone's been sending me letters. A stalker."

If he was surprised by her revelation, Cole didn't waste time remarking on it. "Where are you?"

"Henderson Park. The west side." Her gaze shot to the grassy area in front of her vehicle.

The figure was gone.

She twisted in her seat, trying to figure out where he went, but there was no sign of him. A fresh burst of terror flooded her veins. "Cole, I can't see him. He was right in front of me, but now he's gone."

Had she imagined him?

"Listen to me." Cole's tone was authoritative. "I'm three minutes away. Are your doors locked?"

"Yes." Olivia double-checked them with trembling fingers. Her gaze swept across the park once more, but there was no sign of the shadowy figure. Where had he gone? What kind of game was he playing? As terrifying as it was to have him chasing her, this disappearance act was more frightening. She was trapped in her vehicle without a weapon and with no idea where the danger was.

Lord, please help me.

"Put me on speaker and try to start your car again," Cole ordered.

Shakes overtook her body, but Olivia got the call on speaker. She reached for the keys still hanging in the ignition. Maybe the SUV would start now that she wasn't in a panic. Then something shifted in the corner of Olivia's vision. Her head swiveled.

A shapeless face appeared in the driver's side window, right next to her, dark eyes boring into hers.

She screamed.

TWO

Cole's heart rate spiked. Olivia's scream was bloodcurdling and filled with terror. Then it abruptly cut off as the call dropped.

"Olivia!" He hit redial on his Bluetooth system, and her phone rang, but she didn't answer. Cole pushed the gas pedal to the floor. Trees whipped by as his truck flew down the dark county road. Serenity was a short distance away. Two minutes tops. But a lot could happen in two minutes. He knew from personal experience. His parents died in a heartbeat. One moment there, the next gone. Killed in a motor vehicle accident during a heated argument. He'd been in the back seat and had nearly died too.

Cole dialed Olivia again. Still no answer.

Using voice commands, he ordered his phone to call the Serenity Police Department. He identified himself to dispatch and explained the situation in clipped tones. She assured him officers were en route. Unfortunately, they were on patrol and it would take fifteen minutes to respond. Cole was the closest law enforcement officer. He gripped the steering wheel until it hurt. He'd been to Serenity once before, just passing through, and knew the park was on the opposite side of town.

The seconds clawed at him. They churned his insides and made him want to scream. His grandmother would've told him to pray. Nana's faith was bone-deep, and she'd instilled that same sense of belonging in Cole. Her words of wisdom replayed in his head, as they often did in times of worry.

When you've done all you can, and you feel hopeless, that's when you need prayer the most.

The gas pedal was pushed to the floor. He'd called for backup. Nothing else could be done, so Cole followed his Nana's advice and sent up a winged prayer toward heaven. The weight of responsibility pressed down on his shoulders, his duty as a Texas Ranger made more potent by the fact that he knew Olivia. They weren't friends, more like acquaintances, but she'd impressed him with her quick wit and willingness to go the extra mile. She was also stunningly gorgeous. More than one of his fellow rangers had commented that Cole and Olivia would make a great couple. He'd ignored them. After witnessing the downfall of his parents' marriage, he avoided commitment with every fiber of his being.

Cole blew past the courthouse and the police station on the outskirts of town. The flashing turret lights mounted on the roof of his official state vehicle announced his presence to anyone on the road. Picturesque shops and quaint restaurants lined both sides of the wide street. His focus narrowed to the park up ahead.

Olivia's SUV sat at the far end of the parking lot, the driver's side door facing the playground. Cole shoved his own truck into park while simultaneously reaching for his handgun. His fingers wrapped around the grip, the weapon as familiar as the worn cowboy boots on his feet. There was no sign of Olivia or her attacker. It was likely they were on the other side of the vehicle, near the driver's side door. From his position, Cole didn't have a visual.

On silent footsteps, gun leading the way, he approached. Embedded training slowed his movements even as every cell in his body screamed to hurry. It was reckless to run headlong into an unknown situation. Getting himself shot or killed wouldn't help Olivia.

Wind whipped through the trees, scattering leaves. The frigid cold snaked down the collar of his shirt. Cole barely felt it as he slid up to the rear of Olivia's SUV and peeked around the corner. His breath caught.

The driver's side door of the vehicle was open, the interior light illuminating the empty seat and the surrounding area. Glass sparkled on the asphalt. The window was busted. The attacker had likely broken it in order to open the door and drag Olivia out. But where were they now?

His gaze swept the surrounding area. The nearby street was empty, as was the playground. Could she be inside the vehicle? Dead? It wouldn't have taken long to shoot her.

Heart pounding, Cole eased closer. Olivia's cell phone came into view, resting on the floorboard. More glass littered the seat and the console. But no blood. A momentary blip of relief was shattered by a muffled scream.

He spun. His gaze scanned the park, but the weak streetlights didn't reach the far side. Branches from the ancient oak trees created long shadows big enough to hide an army of men. Walking trails from this area of the park led into a nature preserve, with a lake and more picnic areas. Another muffled scream drifted on the wind. It was drowned out by the sirens of approaching patrol cars. Backup was on the way, but they weren't close enough yet.

On instinct rather than by sight, Cole moved deeper into the park. Scattered leaves drifted across the grass with every gust of wind. Darkness encased him. Self-preservation urged him back. He ignored it. Fear was a tool, but it could also be deadly. It could cause a man to hesitate when he should act, or retreat when he should move forward. Cole had learned a long time ago to disregard his emotions. To maintain control at all times.

There. Shadows shifted to his left. Cole silently moved in that direction and two people took shape. A man wearing all black and something over his face dragged Olivia closer to the walking trails that led into the nature preserve.

"Police!" Cole pointed his weapon at the attacker. "Freeze!"

The man stopped. His head turned and twisted, as if

searching for Cole. He likely couldn't see him in the dark. A faint trickle of moonlight filtering through the tree branches illuminated Olivia's face. Her eyes were wide with terror. The criminal had a hand over her mouth and held a blade to her throat. Liquid trickled down the long column of her neck.

Blood. The sight of it—along with the fear etched on her pretty features—heated Cole's anger. His jaw clenched. He couldn't shoot the man without risking Olivia in the process. "Drop the knife. Now."

For a breath-stealing moment, Cole feared the attacker would slit Olivia's throat right there. But then he pushed her in Cole's direction. She stumbled with the force of the sudden shove. Cole had no choice but to lower his gun to catch her. She sagged in his arms.

Footsteps retreated into the trees. Cole wanted to give chase, but his first priority needed to be Olivia. Was she hurt? In the darkness, it was hard to tell, but her body trembled violently in his arms. Shock was a real possibility. She'd been attacked and nearly kidnapped. The approaching sirens were growing closer, but help was still too far away. Out in the open, Cole and Olivia were sitting ducks if the attacker had a gun on him. Criminals usually had a weapon of choice—this one had used a knife on Olivia—but it would be foolhardy to assume the attacker wasn't carrying more than that.

Cole was not a foolish man.

He hauled Olivia to her feet, but she was shaking too hard to stand. Cole swept his arm under her legs in one smooth move. He didn't turn his back on the woods, but hurried toward the parking lot and the safety of his vehicle.

Olivia clung to him like a burr. Her trembling increased, and with a sudden jolt, Cole realized she was sobbing. He quickened his steps, his heart breaking for her. "I've got you. You're safe now."

"No." she whispered through her tears. "I'm not."

THREE

The Serenity Police Department was a tiny clapboard building across the street from a coffee shop. The tile flooring was chipped, and the walls were painted an industrial gray, but every surface gleamed with cleanliness. A lone officer manned the front desk. Five cubicles served as workstations for officers when they weren't on patrol. An interview room, a kitchen, and the police chief's office completed the first floor. The second was used for storage.

Cole nursed a surprisingly decent cup of coffee and waited for Olivia's interview to be over. Per regulation, they'd given their statements separately. Police Chief Maxwell Sims promised a full update once he had all the information. The two patrol officers on duty were currently searching for the suspect, along with deputies from the county sheriff's office, but there wasn't much to go on. Neither Cole nor Olivia had gotten a good look at the culprit.

The bells over the front door jingled. Texas Ranger Elijah "Eli" Goodwin strolled in. He wore the standard uniform—a white button-down shirt and khakis—but had forgone the usual cowboy hat. His neatly cropped hair was still damp from a recent shower, and he hadn't bothered to shave. Cole's phone call had likely roused him from sleep. They'd been working a high-profile double homicide for the last several days. The case was over now, but it'd meant late nights and early mornings. Shut-eye had been a luxury.

"Aren't you supposed to be on vacation?" Eli demanded in lieu of a greeting as he approached.

Cole flashed him a grin. "Not till tomorrow." He was heading to Corpus Christi to visit his grandmother, who he hadn't seen since before Christmas. Two weeks of home cooking, decent sleep, and a list of handyman repairs awaited him. "In twelve hours, I'll be out of your hair."

Eli rolled his eyes. "I doubt that." The teasing was good-natured and common among their tight-knit group. Eli and Cole were close and often assisted with each other's cases. Eli's expression turned grim. "What happened?"

"Olivia was attacked by an unknown assailant." Cole ran through the little he knew. Since Eli was the Texas Ranger for this area, he would take the lead on any investigation they were involved in. "She said something on the phone about a stalker. Do you know anything about that?"

Shock lifted Eli's brows. "No."

"What about Sienna? Olivia could've confided in her."

Sienna Evans was Eli's fiancée. They were getting married in two weeks, and Olivia was their wedding planner. Cole knew the women were close, and as a private investigator, Sienna would be a good person to ask for help.

Eli shook his head. "Sienna noticed Olivia was stressed, but when she asked her about it, Olivia insisted everything was fine. We figured she simply had a lot on her plate. Olivia's assistant quit three weeks ago, and she hasn't found a replacement, plus she's caring for aging grandparents. That would be a lot for anyone to handle." He huffed out a breath, worry creasing his features. It was clear Eli cared deeply about Olivia. "A stalker? Why didn't she say anything to me?"

"Good question."

The door to the interview room opened. Police Chief Maxwell Sims filled the doorway. Nearly sixty, he had the short, stocky build of an NFL punt returner. His black hair was nearly gray. It contrasted with his sepia-colored skin and black eyes. Faint lines creased the skin on his forehead and a scar dragged the left side of his mouth down. Cole had never worked with the chief, but he'd heard good things from Eli.

The chief greeted Eli with a handshake before turning his attention to Cole. "I'm done taking Olivia's statement. If you don't mind, I'd like to speak to you two in private. Let's go into my office. It'll be more comfortable there."

Cole nodded, his gaze immediately latching on to Olivia as she exited the interview room. Her hair was mussed, caramel-colored strands released from the twist at the back of her neck during the fight with the attacker. She'd also lost her high heels during the struggle. Someone—probably the grandmotherly receptionist manning the front desk—had provided her with a set of flats. A cut marred the creamy skin along the column of her throat and tear tracks streaked her cheeks.

His chest squeezed tight. Without thinking, he closed the distance between them. "Are you okay?"

Her chin trembled, but she straightened her shoulders and nodded. "I'm okay." Liquid warmth filled her sky-blue eyes as she met Cole's gaze. "Thanks to you."

She surprised him by stepping forward and wrapping her arms around his waist for a hug. Cole stiffened for a heartbeat, unaccustomed to such easy affection from someone other than his grandmother. Then he embraced her back. The scent of her perfume—something floral and intoxicating—teased his senses. Without the high heels, Olivia only came up to his shoulder. Her frame fit perfectly against his, causing a jumble of conflicting emotions to war within him. Gratitude that she was safe joined forces with a desire to protect her. And overlaid on top were blaring alarm bells. An internal warning system to keep Olivia at arm's length for his own self-preservation.

He released her and backed away. "Can I call someone for you? A family member?"

"No." She tucked a lock of hair behind her ear. "My

grandparents are visiting friends in Florida until tomorrow. Chief Sims offered to give me a ride home since my vehicle..."

Was part of a crime scene. Cole didn't like thinking about the ways tonight might've gone if Olivia hadn't accidentally called him. He rocked back on his heels. "I should go speak to the chief then, so he can escort you home. Be back in a few minutes."

"Of course."

Cole turned and went into the glass-walled office. Chief Sims was already stationed behind his desk. Eli folded his lean frame into one of the visitor's chairs. Cole elected to stand.

"What do we know so far?" he asked the chief.

"The suspect is still at large." His tight body posture and furrowed brow indicated Chief Sims was very unhappy about that fact. "Unfortunately, there's not much evidence to go on. The perpetrator wore gloves, so there weren't any fingerprints. No witnesses, other than you and Olivia, but unfortunately, neither of you got a good look at the suspect. Whoever he is, he has a basic understanding of cars though. Olivia's SUV was disabled. The perpetrator removed the spark plugs."

Cole whistled. A simple and effective way to ensure Olivia wouldn't be able to escape even if she reached her car. "This was planned."

"Yes. Well-planned." Chief Sims pursed his mouth. "The perpetrator attacked Olivia in the parking lot and dragged her toward the nature preserve. Based on some faint tire treads, it's our belief the culprit parked on the far side of it. Several of the shops on Main Street have cameras. Under normal circumstances, we'd have a view of his vehicle, maybe even a license plate."

"Except he parked on the other side of the preserve, thereby avoiding the cameras." Cole didn't like where this was going. "Olivia mentioned a stalker."

Chief Sims opened a side drawer and removed a file folder. "For the last several weeks, Olivia has received letters from an unknown individual. The first one appeared in her mailbox. Another was slipped under the door of her office. I advised her to get a security system, which she did, for both her home and office. After that, the notes began showing up in different places."

"What places?" Eli asked. He'd taken out a small notepad from his jacket pocket and was scribbling notes.

"In the pew at church. Under the windshield wiper of her car. Nailed to a tree in her backyard."

No wonder Olivia had been terrified. She had reason to be. Cole had worked enough stalking cases to know the perpetrator either escalated or moved on to someone else. In this case, he'd escalated. "The letters increased in frequency?"

"Yes." The chief removed a few sheets of paper. "The letters vary, but follow the same basic pattern of thought. Read one and you've read them all."

He handed one to Eli and offered another to Cole.

My dearest Olivia,

Every time I see you, my heart aches with a

love so intense it consumes me. You plan these beautiful weddings, but the only true beauty is you. Your smile... your laugh... I see them in my dreams. I watch you, and it pains me you don't see me the way I see you. I long for the day you'll recognize our bond and see that we're meant to be. Until then, I'm waiting patiently.

Don't be scared of me, sweetheart. I'm your secret admirer, your guardian. I'm always there, in the shadows, watching over you. My love for you is pure and unyielding. It never ends. And soon... very soon... we'll be together forever.

Your Devoted Admirer

Creepy. Cole's fingers tightened on the letter. "Do you have any suspects?"

"No. Whoever this guy is, he's able to slip in and out of situations without being noticed." The chief scowled. "It's like chasing a ghost."

Cole wasn't buying it. "I'm pretty sure you're dealing with a local, chief. Leaving notes in crowded places is bold. He knows no one will remember him. A stranger would stick out too much. Plus he designed his attack to the security cameras on Main Street. He knew they were there."

"Agreed." Eli studied his copy of the letter again. "Trouble is, I've spent time with Olivia over the last few weeks while planning my wedding and haven't noticed anyone following her. But it's clear this guy is obsessed.

What about an ex-boyfriend? Or even someone she had a casual date with?"

The chief shook his head. "There's no one. Olivia lost her fiancé three years ago in a freak accident." His gaze drifted to the glass on his left. Olivia was pacing the length of the bull pen, her arms wrapped around her midsection. "Aaron was a firefighter. A good man. He was highly allergic to bees and disturbed a hive in his backyard shed. Neighbor found him dead inside the house a few hours later. He'd been stung over 30 times."

Good grief. Judging from the stunned look on Eli's face, he hadn't known about Olivia's fiancé either. Cole was taken aback by the devastating loss Olivia had suffered. And now she was being stalked by a man bent on terrorizing her. "Do you have any suspects at all?"

"Not one. I've taken this case seriously from the get-go. Questioned witnesses, increased patrols in Olivia's neighborhood, and paid a visit to any parolee living in my town that has a record for harassing a female. It's gotten us nowhere. The sheriff's department normally helps on cases like these, but they're stretched thin chasing drug dealers and murderers."

"I'd like to offer my assistance, Chief." Eli frowned. "Honestly, I would've volunteered sooner, but I didn't know Olivia was facing this kind of trouble. She didn't say anything about it."

"I specifically asked her not to mention it to anyone."

Cole was shocked by the lawman's approach. "Why?"

"Because if word got out that a stalker was hunting a

member of our community, there would be nonstop coverage. Olivia would be hounded for information from the townsfolk. Rumor and innuendo would run amuck. It would hinder my investigation, not make it easier."

A burst of anger shot through Cole. He opened his mouth to retort the police chief's logic, but Chief Sims held up a hand to ward him off. "Hold on there, son. I can see the judgment in your eyes, but until tonight, there's been no indication the man stalking her is violent." The chief rubbed his forehead as if a headache was brewing. "Serenity has its problems. We've got drugs. Bar fights and riffraff, same as any other small town. But this kind of thing... an attack and attempted kidnapping... it's never happened during the ten years I've been running this department."

He dropped his hand, his expression worried. "I'm well acquainted with Olivia's family. Her granddaddy was raised here. Her grandmother was a school teacher before retiring. They're good people, and Olivia is their pride and joy. She's all they have left. Mind you, I investigate every case thoroughly, but there are some that hit differently."

Cole's anger faded as the chief's concern for Olivia became evident. His decisions hadn't come from a place of malice. And who was Cole to judge? Before tonight, he'd never stepped foot inside Serenity. Maybe the chief was right, and questioning the locals specifically about a stalker would cause more harm to the investigation than good.

It could also be that the chief was blind to the possibility that a local was involved. Small town law enforcement often had a hard time believing anyone in their community could be twisted enough to engage in murder. Or in this case, stalking.

Cole rocked back on his heels. "I don't often speak for the entirety of Company A, but I second what Eli said. The rangers would be happy to assist in this investigation."

Chief Sims gave him a grateful look. "I'd appreciate any help y'all can provide."

"Excellent." Eli gestured for the file. The Texas Rangers provided assistance to local law enforcement, but except for a few select instances, they had to be invited onto the case. Chief Sims's request made it official. "I'll go over everything you have so far. We'll also have the crime lab put a rush on any evidence collected from tonight's attack. Hopefully, we'll develop a new lead." He glanced at Cole. "Would you mind taking Olivia home?"

Eli wanted Cole to question her. A good idea, since it was likely whoever was behind this was someone Olivia knew. They needed to identify him as soon as possible. Based on tonight's attack, the stalker was getting bolder. It wasn't a question of if he would attack again.

It was a matter of when.

FOUR

Olivia couldn't stop trembling. Months of living in fear coupled with the attack left her exhausted and uncertain.

She was being hunted.

And the man was still out there.

Darkness pressed against the windows of Cole's truck. Olivia buried herself deeper into the passenger seat and absently touched the nick at her neck. She could still feel the blade pressed against her throat, the attacker's hand over her mouth, silencing her screams. He'd broken the window on her SUV before dragging her from the vehicle. Olivia had fought, but not even the skills she'd picked up from a self-defense course had prepared her for the attacker's brute strength. He'd overpowered her easily. It was terrifying to realize just how ill-equipped she was to protect herself.

"Are you warm enough?"

Cole's voice cut through her train of thought, and it took Olivia a moment to process his question. She lowered her hand from her throat. Every vent in the truck was aimed in her direction, warm air blowing across her skin, but it didn't remove the chill deep in her bones. She doubted anything would. Not while her stalker remained free.

Olivia twisted her fingers together and willed herself to stop shaking. "I'm okay."

She glanced at him out of the corner of her eye. His gaze was fixed on the dark country road, his shoulders relaxed, one capable hand manning the steering wheel, the other casually resting on the console between them. Before tonight, they'd been acquaintances. Now, from this day forward, Cole was forever a part of her. He'd saved her life. It was a weird feeling, especially since he was little more than a stranger.

She struggled to come up with something to say. Normally, Olivia was good at making small talk, but after tonight's events, she didn't have it in her. Fortunately, Cole seemed unaffected by the quiet.

The truck's tires hummed against the asphalt. Olivia's head was pounding. She removed the bobby pins from her twist, freeing her hair to relieve some of the pressure before resting against the seat and closing her eyes.

The truck slowed. Olivia winced at the harsh fluorescent lighting pouring through the windshield. This wasn't home. "Where are we?"

"Jax's Burger Joint." Cole pulled into a parking spot and then turned to face her. "We didn't eat dinner. I figured you might be hungry. If not, say the word, and I'll take you straight home."

Her stomach lurched and rumbled as the enticing aroma of french fries ignited hunger pains. Breakfast was a long time ago, and she'd worked through lunch. Food would ease her headache too. Olivia reached for the seat belt release. "A burger would be great."

Cole's lips lifted in a heart-stopping grin. He exited the truck, circling around to open her door for her. Olivia tried not to wince as she used the running board to get out of the truck. Every muscle in her body hurt from struggling against her attacker. She'd be sore tomorrow.

The bell over the door jingled as they entered the all-night diner. Red-and-white striped booths lined the walls and silver-rimmed tables crowded the center. Most of the seats were empty. A waitress wearing an apron over her jeans and T-shirt instructed them to sit where they pleased.

Cole claimed a table with a view of the entire room. "This all right?"

"Fine." She dropped to a chair. Her stomach rumbled loud enough to be heard by the kitchen staff. She blushed and pressed a hand to her midsection. "I'm starving and didn't even realize it."

He chuckled and passed her a menu. "Have you eaten here before?"

"Many times. This is one of my grandpa's favorite restaurants. The burgers are great. So are the chicken wraps." Olivia didn't bother opening the menu. She wanted a cheeseburger with the works and fries, along with a soft drink. Maybe even an ice cream sundae for dessert. The thought brought a wistful smile to her face. "When I was a teen, Grandpa and I would come here and order ice cream sundaes first. Then we'd eat dinner. Grandpa would say it was okay to break the rules now and then, as long as no one got hurt in the process."

"Wise words." Cole studied her over his menu. "Are you a rule follower?"

"I am now. I wasn't as much back then." Olivia had nearly failed out of high school. "I lost my parents, one after the other. Mom died of cancer. Dad had a heart attack a month later. People told me it was from a broken heart. Probably true. He loved my mom something fierce. When I came to live with my grandparents, I was grieving and acted out. It took time, and a lot of patience, but with my grandparents' support, I got through it."

"They sound like wonderful people."

"They're the best." She tilted her head. "What about you? Have any family nearby?"

"Nana, my paternal grandmother, lives in Corpus Christi." He hesitated, and for a moment, Olivia thought that was the only answer she was going to get. Then he said, "My parents died in a car accident when I was eight. Nana raised me."

"I'm sorry. You must miss them." She missed her own parents. Deeply. Grandpa and Granny were amazing. Olivia never wanted for love and affection, but there were times she wondered what her parents would think of her decisions. Would they be proud of her? She hoped so. "What's your grandmother like?"

His lips turned up at the corners. "A firecracker. She's a petite little thing with a backbone of steel and eyes in the back of her head. Nana never took a lick of nonsense from me." His gaze turned distant. "But underneath all that hardness was a warm and caring person. She helped me through a lot after my parents died. More than I can put words to."

"I'm glad you had someone." Olivia laid a hand on his arm. She'd always been an affectionate person, a byproduct of being raised by her big-hearted grandmother. There wasn't a person in the world Granny didn't hug in greeting. "No one should go through grief by themselves. Especially a child."

Cole's gaze met hers. His dark eyes were nearly black, and so often shuttered, but this time, his emotions were laid bare. Sympathy. Understanding. Sadness. They were more similar than either had realized. Teens who'd lost their parents, but had the strength and resilience of grandparents to rely on. That kind of loss shaped you. Changed you. And only someone who had experienced it could relate.

The waitress came, interrupting the moment. She plunked down some water glasses and then took their order before hurrying off.

Olivia undid the wrapper on her straw, dunked it in her ice water, and took a long drink. The liquid soothed her dry throat, but the memory of the blade touching her neck flashed in her mind. As much as she tried to keep the attack at bay, it was never far from her thoughts. "Do you think the man who assaulted me will be found soon?"

The shift in conversation seemed to suit Cole just fine. He straightened in his seat. "We're doing everything we can to make that happen." He tilted his head. "Chief Sims said he purposefully asked you to keep the stalking to yourself."

Olivia nodded. "To be honest, I was relieved. Serenity is a small town with all the perks and difficulties that come with it. Gossip runs rampant, and I had my business to consider. If word got out that I was being stalked..." She shook her head. "It could destroy everything I've built."

"How so?"

"People might be afraid to hire me, fearing they'd be dragged into whatever this mess is. Or worse, they'd blame me for it, as if I'd somehow invited the danger. Most of my business success comes through word of mouth. The last thing I want is the wrong kind of attention."

Blessed Events was her passion and Aaron's legacy. Her event-planning company wouldn't have existed without her fiancé's help. She would walk over hot coals to prevent it from going under. Olivia twirled her straw. "Before tonight, the stalker hadn't done anything except send creepy notes. The attack changes things, and I'm not sure what to do next."

Cole's expression softened. "You don't have to make a decision right now. Eli and the rest of Ranger Company A will assist Chief Sims with the investigation. Hopefully, they'll make progress quickly."

The waitress arrived with their food, interrupting

the conversation. They both said grace and tucked into their meals. The conversation drifted from one topic to another. By the time dinner was over, Olivia learned that Cole loved being a Texas Ranger, watched action movies in his free time, and spent vacations traveling to the best fishing spots in the country. The easy conversation and the food relaxed her. Olivia's headache disappeared.

She leaned back in her chair and rested a hand against her stomach. "Thank you for dinner. I feel much better."

"Good." Cole wiped his mouth with a napkin before tossing it on his empty plate. He hesitated. "I hate to do this, but there are some questions I have about the case."

Olivia figured so. Cozy mysteries took up most of her bookcase, and she'd spent time talking with Sienna about her private investigation company. It was kind of Cole to wait until after dinner though. "I don't know how much I can help you. I've told Chief Sims everything."

"My questions aren't about tonight. They're more general." He shrugged. "This may lead nowhere, but it can often help to have a different person's perspective."

Talking about the stalker threatened to reignite her fear, but Olivia tamped the reaction down. Her fingers played with the cross bracelet on her wrist. A gift from her mother that served as a reminder of God's constant presence in her life. Olivia had faced tough challenges—the loss of her parents and home, the sudden death of her fiancé, the struggle to build her business from the ground up. Through it all, faith had been her touchstone, bringing her comfort during those troubling times. This would be no different.

Olivia straightened her shoulders and took a deep breath before meeting Cole's steady gaze. "Okay. What do you need to know?"

FIVE

Olivia was tougher than Cole had initially given her credit for.

Oh, there had been tears. Terror and shock. All understandable, given what she'd been through. Truth was, Olivia had every reason to collapse under the weight of the events. Instead, she faced them head on with a determination and resolve that was impressive. There was a core of steel behind that beautiful face.

Perhaps it had something to do with God. Olivia seemed to draw strength from playing with the delicate cross bracelet on her wrist. It reminded Cole of his beloved grandmother. Nana had carried a rosary with her at all times. When troubled, she'd pull it from her purse, or the pocket hidden in her soft dress, and run gnarled fingers over the beads. The practiced movements always brought her comfort.

Cole was envious of the depth of their faith. He believed, he prayed. But so often, God seemed far away.

Untouchable. Not the loving and caring Father who provided strength in times of need. The level of trust Nana—and it seemed Olivia—put in the Lord wasn't something he could bring himself to do.

Shoving the notion aside, Cole considered his line of questioning. He hated dragging Olivia through all of this again, but the investigation demanded it. "Chief Sims mentioned you lost your fiancé a few years back."

A shadow crossed her face. "Aaron. He died a little over three years ago."

"Have you dated anyone since then? Even casually?"

She shook her head, the caramel-colored strands running over her shoulders like a silky waterfall. "No." Olivia released the bracelet she'd been playing with. "After Aaron died, I was too grief-stricken. It's only been lately that I've entertained the notion of dating again, but growing my business has been the priority. I barely have time for my grandparents and my friends, let alone a relationship."

Cole considered her answer. It matched what Chief Sims had told them. But it didn't necessarily button up the topic. One of the things Cole did frighteningly well was put himself in a perpetrator's shoes. He thought like a criminal. In this case, like a stalker. The man was obsessed with Olivia. He desired her. And that kind of connection didn't come from afar. His compulsion would drive him close to her. "What about men you've gone out with, even just as friends?"

She frowned. "I don't understand."

"You agreed to have dinner with me earlier. We both

know it wasn't a date, just a friendly meal while we worked on my speech for the wedding. However, your stalker might misinterpret something benign as romantic."

Her eyes widened with understanding. She once again fiddled with the cross pendant on her wrist. "I plan weddings for a living. That puts me in contact with groomsmen, friends, family members. Even if I tried, I doubt I could remember every mild interaction."

She was right. Any one of those men could've interpreted her kindness as flirtation. "Did any of the guys hit on you? Or ask you out?"

Olivia grimaced. "It's possible. I brush that kind of thing off when I'm working. Professionalism is very important to me."

Cole made a mental note to have Olivia review the weddings from the last six months in more detail. The stalking started five weeks ago, so if she interacted with her stalker, it was likely shortly before then. "Do most of the couples you work for live in Serenity?"

"When I was first starting out, yes. Now I'm getting referrals from three counties over. I've been forced to travel a lot for work, which is why it's been hard to make enough time for my grandparents and friends. That's only gotten more difficult since my assistant quit."

Cole remembered Eli mentioning that at the police station. "When did she quit?"

She gave him a pointed look. "*He* quit three weeks ago."

"Your assistant was a man?"

"Yes." Olivia's tone suggested she'd heard derogatory comments from people about that fact. "David was one of the best assistants I've ever had. He worked for me for a year. But then he got engaged to his college sweetheart and moved back to Houston. I was sorry to see him go, but I know the long distance was draining for their relationship."

Cole couldn't imagine spending his days as a wedding planner. He wasn't much for parties to begin with, but weddings in particular often seemed performative. Especially since so many couples divorced a few years later. Others stayed together but were unhappy and constantly fighting, as was the case with his own parents.

He'd been around happily married people—there were several in Company A—but Cole often wondered if those couples would still be together thirty years from now. It was hard to know. There were no guarantees. Which is exactly why he avoided commitment entirely.

Shoving those thoughts aside, he focused on the issue at hand. "What was your relationship with David like?"

"David was my colleague, and I consider him a friend. There was nothing romantic between us. Ever." Olivia's gaze narrowed and a flush rose in her cheeks. "You can't possibly believe he's my stalker."

Cole didn't take offense at her biting tone. She was defending a friend. It made her loyal, albeit misguided. He'd learned a long time ago that everyone had secrets, and many were very good at hiding their true selves from others. Including people who loved and cared for them.

"As far as I'm concerned, we need to consider everyone a suspect. Including David."

She arched a brow. "Are you going to accuse my pastor too? What about my elderly neighbor next door?"

He shrugged. "If I have to." Cole met her heated gaze with his own. "I'll do whatever is necessary to sort this out."

The determination coursing through him must've been reflected in his expression, because Olivia released a breath and her shoulders dropped. She rubbed her forehead. "I'm sorry. Of course, you're only trying to help." She sighed. "I don't want to believe that whoever is behind this is someone I know well."

Sympathy stabbed at him. Cole had been accused of letting persistence run roughshod over people's feelings before. Last year, he nearly lost Eli as a friend by accusing Sienna of lying about a murder case. It turned out she was telling the truth. After apologizing, Cole and Eli had smoothed things over, but the painful lesson lingered. He couldn't let his naturally suspicious nature color a case. Sometimes, things were just what they seemed to be.

Maybe Olivia was right, and David was a true friend. Time—and an investigation—would reveal that. But until there was a reason to doubt Olivia's impressions, Cole should be gentler in his approach. "No, I'm sorry. I shouldn't have pushed so hard."

She gave him a weak smile. "Can we finish this conversation tomorrow? I'm tired."

"Of course." He picked up the bill. "It's been a long night. Let's get you home."

Cole settled up with the cashier. The night air was frosty as they exited the restaurant. His gaze scanned the parking lot, senses on high alert for any sign of danger, but nothing stirred. Still, he wouldn't let down his guard. Not for a moment.

Olivia was quiet during the short drive to her home. Cole sensed she was pondering their conversation. He gave her the space to think. His own thoughts were a jumble and needed sorting out. Days of little sleep had left his emotions on edge. That was the only explanation for this increasing sense of awareness when it came to the beautiful woman sitting next to him. Her perfume teased his senses, and he wrestled with the urge to take her hand. To comfort her, as she'd so easily done to him in the diner when they'd discussed his parents.

Cole rarely talked about his family. The words had come easily with Olivia though. Probably because she'd spoken openly about her own loss. There was a connection there, but it went deeper than that. The kindness she'd demonstrated... the easy affection... it did something to him. Something scary and yet captivating all at the same time. Cole didn't know whether to run from her or lean closer.

Dangerous thoughts. He'd take Olivia home, report back what he'd learned to Eli, and then head to Corpus Christi in the morning. Some distance—and a good night's sleep—would fix everything.

The GPS steered Cole to a small clapboard house

with a trim yard and a cheery yellow mailbox. An iron bench rested under the branches of a large elm tree. He retrieved Olivia's laptop bag from the seat—Chief Sims had returned it to her after she'd dropped it running from the attacker—and circled the vehicle to open her door. She winced slightly while getting down.

Cole took her elbow. "I'll walk you to the door."

"Actually, I need to check my grandparents' mailbox first." She gestured to the house across the street. "I meant to do it yesterday and forgot."

"I'll go. Wait here." He crossed the street to save her the steps, since it was clear she was in pain. Her grandparents lived in a custom-built home with charming shutters and a two-car garage with an added storage space on top.

The mailbox squeaked when he opened it. Flyers and envelopes were stuffed inside. Cole freed the items. An owl hooted overhead. The hair on the back of Cole's neck rose, and he turned. Olivia was standing at the end of the driveway, the moonlight painting her beauty with an ephemeral glow. The rest of the street was silent. Yet Cole couldn't shake the notion that he was being watched.

No. Not him.

Olivia.

Mentally cursing himself for not taking her straight inside before getting the mail, Cole closed the distance between them on long strides. "Here's the mail." He handed the stack to her before taking her elbow again and guiding her up the walkway. His gaze shifted right and left. Nothing stirred. Cole wondered if he was simply imagining things. "Is that an apartment over your grandparents' garage?"

Olivia nodded, removing her keys from her jacket pocket. "They built it years ago, and rent it out for extra money."

"Anyone living in it now?"

"No. David was the last person to live there. He moved back to Houston a few weeks ago."

Cole glanced over his shoulder at the darkened windows. He'd do a perimeter check. It was possible someone had broken into the apartment while Olivia's grandparents were away.

Beside him, Olivia inhaled sharply. Cole's attention immediately went to her and then the door. "What is it?"

"The door was unlocked." She trembled. "And my alarm isn't beeping like it should."

Cole's hand flew to his weapon. He was tempted to go inside and search the house, but his primary objective was keeping Olivia safe. Without a word, he gestured for her to move behind him. Together, as one unit, they backed away from the house toward his truck.

He needed to get her out of here.

Before the stalker made his next move.

SIX

The next morning, Olivia added a generous amount of hazelnut creamer to her coffee. She'd barely slept a wink last night. After escaping in Cole's truck, Chief Sims responded to check Olivia's home. Someone had broken in, but nothing was touched. Her safety compromised, she'd stayed at her grandparents' house in the guest bedroom last night.

Exhaustion and stress threatened to pull her back to bed, but hiding under the covers wasn't an option. Instead, she'd use coffee and sugar to get through the day. She stood on her tiptoes to reach the extra plates at the top of her grandmother's cabinet. Warmth at her back alerted her to Cole's presence one second before a set of powerful hands took the plates away from her. "Let me help with those."

She met his dark-eyed gaze and her heart skipped a beat. Cole hadn't left her side since the attack in the park. Last night, he'd stayed in the apartment over the garage and kept watch on the property. Something Olivia was grateful for. The break-in at her house had left her shaken and feeling vulnerable. Knowing he was nearby kept the worst of her fears at bay.

Today, he was dressed in a freshly pressed light-blue shirt and khakis. His firm jaw was clean-shaven. According to Cole, rangers were often called out to crime scenes unexpectedly. He kept an emergency bag with clothes and other toiletries in his vehicle.

Cole carried the plates to the table. Olivia picked up her mug again and took a long sip of coffee, willing the caffeine into her system.

"Based on my experience, the intruder used a wireless jammer to disarm Olivia's security system." Eli scowled, his dark brows drawing down over his eyes. "Unfortunately, they're surprisingly easy to purchase online."

Sienna Evans was nestled in the breakfast nook next to her fiancé. Her hair was a tangle of curls, and she was dressed comfortably in jeans and a soft sweater that highlighted the pink color in her cheeks. Concern and sympathy warmed her expression as Olivia claimed a seat at the table. The private investigator was no stranger to having her life threatened. Last year, she'd nearly been killed.

Olivia selected a bear claw from the box of pastries in the center of the table. "It doesn't make sense. Why break in to my house at all? He didn't steal anything. Didn't leave a note."

Cole and Eli shared a look.

Olivia wiped icing off her fingers, her stomach sinking. "What?"

Sienna was the one who answered, her tone gentle. "He was probably lying in wait for you, Liv."

Her words were like an icy bucket of sludge. Olivia gripped the paper napkin hard enough to turn her knuckles white. She didn't want to believe her friend, but it was a logical conclusion. If sleep hadn't robbed her of brain cells, she might've figured it out on her own. Her gaze swung to Cole. "He was there when we arrived?"

"That's my suspicion." Cole had selected a blueberry muffin from the box, but it sat untouched on his plate. "He must've booked it after we left, because when Chief Sims arrived to sweep the house, it was empty."

"There's another possibility." Eli gestured for the orange juice, and Sienna passed it to him. "The stalker may have simply broken into the house to scare Olivia. To demonstrate that her security system was ineffective. I'm sure when Cole arrived in the park and Olivia escaped, he was angry. Breaking into the house reasserts his control."

Olivia didn't know which option was worse. Did it even matter? Whoever was after her had invaded her privacy and threatened her life. Fear tangled with anger. "I need to get a better security system. One that can't be bypassed with a wireless jammer."

"I know a company that can help with that." Sienna broke off a piece of her scone. "We can install one in your grandparents' home too. In the meantime, we need to ensure your safety."

"How?"

"You could go away for a while," Cole suggested. "Your grandparents are in Florida on vacation. Join them."

She'd tossed and turned all night, considering her options. None of them were good, but leaving was too costly. "I can't do that. I have commitments. A business to run."

His brows arched. "You're going to plan weddings with a stalker chasing you?"

"I've been doing it for the last five weeks, thank you very much." Her cheeks heated, and although she knew her tone was snappy, exhaustion and stress prevented her from reeling it in. "I can't simply pack up and leave on vacation. I signed contracts with my clients and there are penalties for breaking them. This man—whoever he is—has stolen my sense of safety. I refuse to allow him to destroy the business I've built for the last three years."

Her argument struck a chord with Cole, because a flush crept up his neck and his mouth opened as if he was preparing to give her a lecture of his own. Sienna held up a hand before he could get a word out though. "Olivia's right. Right now, we don't have a clear suspect."

"What about David, her old assistant?"

"Guy checks out." Eli took a sip of his coffee. "Houston Police Department officers spoke to David this morning. He was at home with his mom all night. She confirmed it."

"Like I said, no clear suspect," Sienna continued, as if she'd never been interrupted. "Nor can we be sure that sending Olivia to Florida will keep her safe. Her stalker may simply follow her there, and then she'll be on her own with her grandparents. At least here she has people who can help protect her."

Cole's mouth snapped closed, and he sat back in his seat. "So what do you suggest? Whoever the stalker is, he's determined. He's come after Olivia twice and proven to be tech savvy. A new security system will help, but it won't protect her when she's outside her home."

"That's where you come in," Sienna said.

His brows winged up. "Me?"

Sienna broke off another piece of her scone. Olivia recognized the calculated look in her friend's eyes. It'd been there when negotiating with the caterer and photographer. The woman understood people and knew how to convince them to do as she wanted. "You can go undercover, Cole. As Olivia's new assistant."

Silence followed the declaration. Olivia's gaze shifted to Cole. He looked as stunned as she felt.

"It's the perfect solution." Eli focused on Cole. Clearly the couple had discussed this on the car ride over. "The only people in town who know your true identity are the police chief and the receptionist. I'm sure they'll keep quiet. Olivia will have 24-hour protection and you can assess the situation. We know her stalker is likely someone from Serenity, but we don't have any solid suspects. With your law-enforcement training, you'll be able to spot anyone acting strange."

Olivia realized Eli was right. After the attack at the park, Cole drove her straight to the police station. The only people there were Chief Sims and the receptionist. And then again last night, when the intruder broke into her house, Chief Sims responded to the call. No other members of law enforcement interacted with Cole.

"It'll never work." Cole's mouth flattened into a thin line. "I confronted the stalker last night in the park."

"It was dark," Eli argued. "And you said yourself the perpetrator didn't get a good look at you."

A muscle in Cole's jaw clenched. The flush that'd started at his neck during the harsh exchange with Olivia was now in his cheeks. It was obvious he was unhappy about the plan. He shot daggers in Eli's direction and then stood. "I need a word in private with you."

Olivia watched silently as the two men went out on the porch. Cole closed the back door a bit too hard and the window panes rattled. She winced, then rose from her chair. "I should intervene. Cole has been incredibly generous with his time, but he can't put his life on hold to play bodyguard. He has plans with his grandmother. If he doesn't want to go along with the plan, then he shouldn't feel forced to."

Sienna grabbed her arm. "Don't you dare. Rangers are used to putting their personal lives on hold, and going undercover solves multiple problems. You're safe enough to continue working, and Cole can identify potential suspects. Let him discuss it with Eli. Cole will realize it's the right thing to do."

Olivia wanted to argue, but fear held her tongue. Last night's attack in the park, and the home invasion, proved she was vulnerable. Cole's actions had been the only thing that saved her. She wasn't foolish enough to throw away his help to save her pride.

Still, it hurt that he'd fought so adamantly against being her bodyguard.

More than she wanted to admit.

SEVEN

The brisk air cooled Cole's heated skin but did little to assuage his temper. He didn't take kindly to being handled. Sienna and Eli had come up with this plan and hadn't had the decency to present it to him first before involving Olivia. It left Cole in a terrible position. He marched to the edge of the porch before turning to face his friend. "This is a bad idea."

Eli leaned against the porch railing, crossing his arms over his chest. "Why is that?"

His nonchalant attitude only fueled the flames of Cole's anger. "The stalker has gone after Olivia twice in less than 24 hours. How can I guarantee her safety in an uncontrolled environment with hundreds of people, like a wedding reception? It's impossible."

"The stalker hasn't approached Olivia in a crowded environment. He's purposely waited until she was by herself."

"So far. That doesn't mean he won't get desperate

enough to try it." Cole threw up his hands in frustration. "Come on, Eli. You've worked enough of these cases to realize the risk. Do you really believe Olivia understands the gamble she's taking with her life?"

"I think she's made her viewpoint clear. She's been dealing with this for weeks and is unwilling to let the stalker destroy her business. I can't say I blame her. Olivia has worked tirelessly for her success. I would make the same choice in her shoes." He leveled a hard look in Cole's direction. "And I think if you're honest with yourself, you would too."

Cole's jaw clenched. He wanted to refute Eli's last comment, but couldn't. He'd choose to face the danger rather than run and hide. But he was also a trained Texas Ranger. She was a wedding planner, for heaven's sake. Olivia lived in a happy bubble of flower arrangements and color charts, not the gritty and hardened world of criminals. "If going away isn't an option, then install the new security system and have her take a week off work. That'll give you time to investigate more fully."

"Except we have nothing to go on. No fingerprints, no DNA, no witnesses. The letters are written on card stock that's available in dozens of stores." Eli shrugged. "Even if I worked nonstop on this case, it wouldn't help."

Cole spun and planted his hands on the porch railing. The wood bit into his palms. The backyard was an oasis of flowers and greenery. A hammock under a pecan tree begged to be slept in. Birds flitted from branches to the feeders tucked among the plants. There was even one for hummingbirds.

He drew in a breath, searching for a rational argument among the turbulent thoughts running amok in his mind. This wasn't like him. Emotional and uncertain. But the idea of Olivia placing herself in danger twisted him into knots. He didn't want her to get hurt. And he was terrified he wouldn't be able to keep her safe.

Eli sighed. "Is this about your grandmother? Is there something wrong?"

"No. Nana's fine."

"Will she be upset if you cancel on her?"

He snorted. "Not for this. She'd come here and give me a kick in the pants for refusing to protect Olivia." He drew in another breath. The scent of the roses, blooming even in these chilly temperatures, filled his nose. "It's the responsibility, Eli. Working a case is one thing. But being Olivia's bodyguard... that's something else entirely. I don't want to screw up."

His friend was quiet for a long moment. "I get that. When Sienna's life was threatened, I was terrified things would spiral out of control. But then I realized it didn't matter. The stubborn woman was going to go after the killer, whether I was by her side or not. At least if I was with her, she had someone watching her back."

Cole remembered Eli's dedication. At the time, he'd considered it foolhardy. Now he realized how admirable it was. "So you're saying Olivia is going to work, regardless. I might as well be there to protect her."

"She's made up her mind. Given the circumstances, I don't think it's an unreasonable decision. If things change, we can adjust the plan. This isn't written in stone."

Eli was right. Olivia wasn't being irrational, and it wasn't his job to hold her hostage in her own home.

"There's something else you should consider," Eli continued. "Both attacks happened when the stalker believed Olivia was alone. If you're by her side, that may be enough to prevent him from coming after her again, and as her assistant, you'll have access to everyone she's interacting with. This gives us the best chance to find a lead on her stalker's identity."

It was a good argument. Cole believed the perpetrator was someone Olivia knew. Probably someone she talked to regularly. As much as he hated to admit it, the plan was an excellent one. And honestly, could he really walk away? If Olivia got hurt because he refused to protect her, Cole would never forgive himself.

Decision made, he began strategizing a plan. "Lieutenant Rodriguez needs to be informed."

Their boss wouldn't take kindly to being kept out of the loop. Lieutenant Vikki Rodriguez ran Company A with a no-nonsense attitude that permeated their entire unit. She was strict when necessary, but had a heart of gold. Every one of the rangers respected her.

"So does Chief Sims," Cole continued. "I can protect Olivia, but not officially as a Texas Ranger. This has to be done on my own time."

It was the only way he could dedicate all his energy and resources. A fact Eli and Sienna were well aware of. Since Cole was on vacation, he wouldn't be asked to work another case. He'd be available to protect Olivia twenty-four/seven.

Cole straightened and then turned to face his fellow ranger. "We have two weeks to figure this out."

"Yep." Eli grinned. "Heaven knows, we love a challenge."

Cole snorted. "Just don't get mad at me if I don't have a speech prepared for your wedding."

"Oh, no. I'm holding you to that agreement. You'll be spending hours with Olivia as her new assistant. She can help you."

His nose wrinkled. "I hate weddings. And I don't know the first thing about event planning."

Eli laughed. "I don't think Olivia will care." The smile faded from his face. "I've already requested Jackson's help on the case. Felicity may join in too."

Jackson Barker was an excellent ranger with a keen eye for details. So was Felicity Capshaw. Cole had worked with both of them at one time or another. They'd be an asset to have, especially since Eli was getting married in two weeks. If they didn't wrap this case up by then, Jackson would take the lead so Eli could go on his honeymoon.

"I can live in the garage apartment above her grandparents and keep an eye on her when we aren't working," Cole said.

"I would suggest Olivia to stay with her grandparents. They come back from their vacation today. This guy has been very careful, and he seems worried about getting caught. Having more people around her may serve an extra layer of protection."

Cole nodded, even as fresh worry crowded his mind. He'd be with Olivia twenty-four, seven. Potentially for weeks. An uncomfortable proposition given the intense hum of attraction riding under the surface of their interactions. He liked her. More than he wanted to. And that was dangerous. Especially now that he was charged with protecting her. Distractions could prove deadly. He needed to make sure his head was clear, which meant locking down these emotions.

It was something Cole had experience with. During his parents' turbulent marriage, he'd drifted through the house like a ghost, doing his best to avoid triggering another bout of screaming. Wants and needs didn't matter. His feelings didn't matter. All that mattered was surviving the war zone. It'd taken years—along with therapy and prayer—to heal those wounds after his parents' death. Nana had been an immense help, her love and support, and calm demeanor, a balm to his hurt. Cole didn't lock up his feelings anymore, but he retained the skill. Now was a good time to implement it.

The two men went back inside the kitchen. Olivia glanced up. She'd schooled her features into a mask of indifference, but Cole saw the hope in her eyes. Any doubts about his decision evaporated. He couldn't leave her alone to face this. For better or worse, he was in this.

He unpinned the ranger badge from his shirt and then held out his hand to Olivia. "Hi. I'm Cole, your new assistant."

She hesitated, and then her lips curved into a smile. "Welcome to the team."

As Olivia's hand slid into his, a spark coursed straight through him. Cole was annoyed that he hadn't managed to avoid the reaction. *Lock it down, Donnelly.* This stupid attraction had to stop. He'd been around beautiful women before and it'd never been a problem. This time wouldn't be any different.

He'd make sure of it.

EIGHT

Olivia snuck a glance at Cole from behind her sunglasses. They'd spent the morning with Eli and Sienna, strategizing the best way to handle any new leads that came from his role as her assistant. Whatever objections Cole had to the plan prior to his talk with Eli seemed to have dissipated. He'd spoken to his boss. Chief Sims had also been informed and given his approval. Everything was set to go. So why did she feel so nervous? Probably because lying didn't come easily to her.

As Cole's truck turned onto Main Street, and Olivia's office came into view, her pulse jumped. "My secretary, Susan, is a real sweetheart, but she's also a gossip. Make sure you stick to the story we came up with. And don't get offended if she grills you about your family and other personal stuff."

"Relax, Olivia. I know how to handle myself."

She flicked another glance in his direction and snorted. "You know how to handle murderers and home-grown terrorists. I seriously doubt you know how to manage a seating chart or an interfering mother-in-law."

His lips curved up. "You got me there. But I'm not an ogre you've let out of his cage. I can be charming when the need arises. Besides, being new to the event-planning business is part of my cover story. No one will expect me to know how to handle those things."

"True, but..." She drummed her nails on the door, considering her options. Cole was a strong-willed lawman used to calling the shots. While Olivia understood his role was to flush out her stalker, she didn't want him forcefully questioning her clients and causing issues in the process. "I'm worried."

She needed to tell him. To explain just why Blessed Events meant so much to her.

Olivia stopped drumming her nails abruptly. "I've poured everything I have into the business. And not just because it's mine. It's..." A lump formed in her throat. "Aaron gifted Blessed Events to me."

Cole pulled into a parking spot near her office and shoved the truck into gear before turning to face her. "I don't understand. I thought Aaron was a firefighter."

"He was." She took a breath to steady her emotions, her attention drifting to the small shop with her company logo in the window. "Blessed Events was my dream, one I discussed with him the entire time we were dating. After we got engaged, and unknown to me, Aaron hired a lawyer to draw up the business paperwork. I was the owner, but he poured most of his life savings into the business bank account."

A tear made its way down her cheek and Olivia swiped at it. She'd cried so much in the months after Aaron died. But grief was a strange thing. It lay hidden inside until a memory unleashed it. And then suddenly the pain was as fierce and as fresh as ever. "It was my wedding present. Aaron intended to gift it early, but he never got the chance to."

"Because he died?"

She nodded. "The day after he passed, the lawyer called me into his office and explained everything. I was shocked. But after the heartbreak wore off, I became determined to make Blessed Events a success." Olivia swiped at another tear. "Aaron believed in me. I didn't want to let him down."

Thinking about those days brought back a wave of memories. Aaron's funeral had been attended by the entire town. And then, in the parking lot after the event, Olivia had an encounter with Aaron's younger brother, Justin. He'd found out about the money Aaron left to her and was furious. Despite her attempts to explain, Justin had reacted with violence.

He'd assaulted her in the parking lot. Officers arrested him and uncovered a large amount of opioids— enough for a drug distribution charge. Justin was currently serving out a fifteen year sentence.

Cole sat back in his seat and blew out a breath. "Aaron sounds like a wonderful guy. It must've been very difficult to lose him."

"It was. I wanted to hide away from the world, but couldn't, so I kept putting one foot in front of the other until things weren't so bleak." Olivia turned to face him. "I need you to understand. I'm protective of my business because it's my livelihood, yes, but it's more than that. It's the last gift Aaron ever gave me. I know you believe my stalker is someone I know, and you have a job to do, but discretion is important."

He was silent, his gaze fixed on the happenings beyond the windshield. Foot traffic was light. A mother pushed a stroller toward the park. An elderly couple, bundled in jackets, walked hand in hand toward the general store.

Olivia tried to read Cole's expression, but it was a blank slate. Whatever he was thinking was a mystery. "I hope that doesn't come across as ungrateful. I appreciate everything you're doing—"

"It's not ungrateful at all." He fell back into silence for several heartbeats. Then he turned to face her. "In fact, I owe you an apology. I wasn't thrilled about the undercover bodyguard idea. But I was wrong."

His gaze met hers and the understanding in them stole her breath. "This encounter feels divinely guided. What are the chances I would be the one to save you last night? Now you need a bodyguard and I happen to be going on vacation at just the right time. Lots of people would see those events as coincidental, but my Nana taught me that God works through opportunities. He pushes us in the right direction." His mouth quirked. "I'm not very good at listening sometimes."

She was touched by his vulnerability. Olivia had wrestled with her own faith from time to time. Following

God's guidance didn't always come easily. "Well, to be fair, you're giving up time with your grandmother. And much needed rest. I'd probably have a few words with God about that too."

He laughed. The sound was a deep rumble, and his broad smile was endearing. She liked it.

Cole's expression grew serious again. "Keeping you safe is my top priority—that won't change—but I promise to use as much discretion as I can. However, a situation may occur that requires immediate action. You have to listen and do as I say without question."

It wasn't an unreasonable request. Cole's job was to protect her and flush out the stalker. If he thought there was danger, she needed to rely on his training. Olivia nodded. "That's fair."

"Good. Then it's a deal."

"Thank you." She placed a hand on his forearm, the hard muscles firm against her palm. Heat from his skin seeped through his shirtsleeve. "I truly appreciate everything you're doing to protect me. Especially since you gave up vacation time with your grandmother."

"Nana will understand. It's not the first time I've had to cancel on her." Cole placed his hand over hers. The strong fingers encased her smaller ones, making Olivia feel dainty and feminine. Warmth slid up her arm into her belly. Butterflies ignited as a heat crept into her cheeks. "I'm glad I'm here to help. We'll catch this guy, Olivia. In the meantime, we'll have plenty of opportunities to work on my speech for Eli's wedding."

A laugh bubbled up. "That's true."

He squeezed her hand and then released it. "Ready to do this?"

She nodded, feeling like a pile of bricks had been lifted from her shoulders. Her stalker was still out there somewhere, but for the first time since this entire thing began, Olivia was hopeful.

Those positive vibes continued as they crossed Main Street. The sunshine was warm on Olivia's hair and the air was scented with sugar from the bakery. Mr. Kemp, the town barber, waved in greeting from the doorway of his shop three doors down. Olivia waved back.

"Friendly town." Cole also lifted his hand in a greeting to Mr. Kemp. "I can see why you enjoy living here."

"My recent troubles aside, Serenity is a great place to be. The townsfolk take care of each other." She entered Blessed Events. The front room had a desk for her secretary and a waiting area for clients. Matching love seats were arranged around a coffee table loaded with wedding magazines. Fresh flowers scented the air.

"Morning!" Susan Reynolds rose from her white desk chair. Bangles on her wrist jangled and her long dress fluttered around her legs as she circled the desk. Her curly hair hit just above the shoulders and framed her heart-shaped face. She grabbed a stack of message slips and handed them to Olivia. "There's nothing urgent in there, but you should return those calls before lunch. You've got back-to-back meetings with new clients this afternoon. I need you to look over the Clemming budget and there are half a dozen invoices on your desk for review. Oh, and you have a cake tasting at five."

The day was off to a jump start.

"Thanks for taking care of everything this morning."

Olivia hadn't told Susan about the creepy messages or the attack from last night. Chief Sims wanted to continue keeping things as quiet as possible for now. Eli concurred, especially since Cole was working undercover. The fewer questions about his sudden appearance, the better. Olivia felt uneasy about the decision since Susan worked for her, but Chief Sims assured her it was the correct way to handle the situation. Gossip and rumors could alert the stalker to their plan, which might cause him to go into hiding or escalate in a panic. Neither would be good.

Olivia gestured to Cole. "Susan, I'd like you to meet Cole Donnelly. He's the new assistant I hired yesterday."

"Welcome." Susan's gaze seemed to assess Cole in a flash, and judging from her broad smile, she liked him.

A relief. Susan had never been a fan of Olivia's former assistant, David. They'd been too different. Susan was thirty and married. Her husband worked construction, and they hung out with a blue-collar crowd. She prided herself on organization and tidiness. David was mid-twenties, from a wealthy background, and single. He'd been artistic, messy, and a touch snobbish. Eventually they'd formed a cordial working relationship, but it'd taken time.

"Pleasure to meet you, ma'am." Cole tipped his cowboy hat in her direction. "Olivia said the office couldn't run without you. I worked in a hotel in Galveston before this, so I'm new to the wedding-planning business. I hope you won't hold it against me if it takes some time to learn the ropes."

"Nonsense. You have a smart look about you, cowboy. I'm sure we'll get along fine." Susan flashed him a brilliant smile. It wasn't flirty. More endearing, like he was the long-lost brother she'd dreamed of. "Olivia mentioned you're a good friend of Elijah Goodwin."

"Yes, ma'am. We go way back."

They'd stuck as close to the truth as possible when creating Cole's cover story. Olivia watched as the two continued to talk. Susan was normally tough as nails and suspicious of newcomers. Cole proved to be an exception. True to his word, he charmed her. Or maybe it was the connection to Elijah and Sienna that convinced Susan to give Cole a chance. She adored the couple as much as Olivia did.

Leaving them to their conversation, Olivia went to her office. The walls were painted a pale lavender. A stack of mail and invoices rested on the corner of her glass-topped desk. She opened her laptop to power it up before shuffling through the bills.

"You're right." Cole appeared in the doorway. He glanced over his shoulder and lowered his voice. "Susan grilled me about my family."

Olivia chuckled. "I warned you." She gestured to the desk on the other side of the office. It was equipped with a PC, a phone, and a comfy leather chair. "That's yours."

"Perfect." He assessed the mood boards leaning against the wall. "I'll need a list of your clients."

"To learn about them? Or to do a background check?"

He flashed her a charming smile. "Both." His nose wrinkled. "It's illegal to access law enforcement databases for personal purposes, and since I'm working this case on my own time, I have to be creative. But you'd be surprised what can be dug up using public resources and social media. If I find anyone suspicious, I'll turn the name over to Eli and he'll do an official background check."

Olivia prayed Cole wouldn't find anyone suspicious among her clients. The thought that one of them was stalking her... a shudder rippled down her spine. "I'll have Susan get you a list."

A manila envelope in the stack of mail caught her attention. Her name was scrawled across it, but there were no stamps. It hadn't been mailed. She picked it up, feeling the weight and unusual shape at the bottom. One of her clients was supposed to drop off a sample of the decorations she wanted for the reception table center-pieces. This must be it.

She unsealed the back flap and glanced inside the envelope. Confusion gave way to horror as she realized what was staring back at her.

NINE

Cole's stomach turned as Chief Sims lifted the dead mouse out of the envelope. A noose had been tied around the rodent's neck. The body was stiff, indicating it'd been dead for a while.

It was his first good look at the stalker's handiwork. After Olivia discovered what was inside the envelope, Cole left everything as it was for Chief Sims. Although he was a Texas Ranger and knew how to preserve evidence, he wasn't officially working this case. Any improper handling of the contents could damage precious evidence or give a defense attorney an opening to challenge the validity.

Cole wouldn't take any chances. Not with Olivia's life on the line.

Chief Sims grimaced as he studied the dead rodent. "This doesn't look like a field mouse. It probably came from a pet shop. There's a place off the freeway that caters to people who own snakes."

"Ugh." Olivia wrapped her arms around her midsection. "I can't imagine owning a snake as a pet, let alone feeding it a live mouse." Color rose in her cheeks as she eyed the mouse dangling from the noose held by Chief Sims. She'd initially been shocked by the envelope's contents. That seemed to have shifted to indignation, judging from the spark in her eyes. "That poor creature was tortured."

"Yes, he was." Chief Sims's tone was tight with restrained anger. He slipped the rodent into an evidence bag. Then he carefully pulled out a piece of paper from inside the envelope.

Cole stepped closer to read it.

Dearest Olivia,

Did you really think you could escape so easily? Our little game has just begun. Like this mouse couldn't escape its fate, neither can you. I'm always watching, always close by, waiting for the right moment. I look forward to our next encounter with an anticipation that grows stronger every day.

Your Devoted Admirer

Beside him, Olivia stiffened. Cole instinctively placed a reassuring hand on the small of her back. She leaned into the touch, her shoulder brushing his. That simple contact sent a wave of awareness through him, firing up his protective nature.

Their conversation in the truck earlier this morning had shifted something for Cole. He didn't know what exactly. All he knew was that Olivia's love and dedication to Aaron was admirable. She'd suffered a great loss and yet persevered. More than that, she'd done it with grace.

Cole often dealt with the worst of humanity in his job. His childhood—and his parents' difficult marriage—had laid the groundwork for his jaded nature. But every once in a while, someone came along and knocked down his preconceived notions. Olivia was one of those people. What did it mean? Cole didn't know. It was his duty to protect her, but this was starting to feel less like obligation and more like need.

Divinely inspired. That's what Nana would say, and Cole was in no position to argue with that logic. The coincidences were too many to be anything less. There hadn't been many times he'd felt God's hand directing him. More often than not, Cole found himself on an empty sea, drifting through life without an anchor to hold him steady. But every once in a while—like now—even he couldn't miss the Lord's obvious guidance.

Shoving those thoughts aside, Cole read through the note again. "This one is just like the others. Handwritten in block lettering, but it's shorter than the previous letters. There's also an edge of desperation to it."

Chief Sims nodded. "This is a warning."

"What does that mean?" Olivia asked, her gaze bouncing between the two men.

Cole hesitated. He didn't want to scare her any more than she already was, but this was her life on the line. She deserved to know the risk. "The initial attack on you was well-planned. He'd likely been thinking about it for weeks, only to have it fail. Then he broke into your house and that didn't work either. Now he's angry. More than likely, he's already making plans for his next attack."

Olivia's jaw clenched as she stared at the bag with the dead mouse. "And this time, if he's successful, he's going to make me pay for escaping."

Cole stepped into her line of sight and dipped down until they were eye-to-eye. "That's not going to happen. In order to get to you, he has to go through me. Despite what Eli may have told you..." He flexed an arm. "I'm tougher than I look."

That comment earned him a smile, just as he'd hoped it would. Gratitude, enough to warm Cole straight through, erased the fear and worry shining in her sky-blue eyes. "I'm gonna have you open the mail from now on."

"Good idea. I'm not scared of a dead mouse."

She lifted a brow. "What about a live one?"

"Let's not talk about that."

She smothered a laugh. All joking aside, Cole had already decided he'd be opening the mail from now on. If only to spare Olivia the ordeal of coming across another ugly message. Whatever happened, she wasn't in this by herself. And Cole had no intention of letting anyone harm her.

Chief Sims tucked the letter into another evidence bag. "When was this delivered?"

"According to Susan, it was dropped off by Mr. Kemp, the barber, just after nine this morning." The mirth left Olivia's expression as quickly as it'd appeared. "Someone put the envelope in his mail slot after closing yesterday or in the early-morning hours."

Cole pointed to Olivia's name scrawled on the front. "Mr. Kemp saw the envelope wasn't addressed to him and figured someone had simply mixed up the stores. He brought it over. I reviewed the surveillance footage from Olivia's cameras and it confirms Susan's story." He extended a USB drive toward the chief. "I took the liberty of making a copy for you."

"Thanks." Chief Sims labeled another evidence bag and dropped the item inside. "Unfortunately the barber shop doesn't have any security cameras. Which is probably why the perpetrator delivered the envelope there instead of slipping it directly into Olivia's mail slot."

The stalker was angry, but not enough to make a sloppy mistake. "It supports our theory that the stalker is a local. He knows which stores have cameras and which don't."

The chief grunted. It was clear he didn't like the idea that someone from Serenity was involved. "Any progress on suspects?"

"Not yet, but I haven't dug into any of Olivia's clients yet."

"Let me know if you find anything." Chief Sims picked up the evidence bags and then pegged both Cole and Olivia with a grandfatherly look. "Be careful, you two. I have a bad feeling about this."

Cole didn't say it, but he shared the police chief's feelings. The stalker's note had put them on alert.

This wasn't over. Not by a long shot.

TEN

The rest of the day flew by quickly. While Cole tackled background checks, Olivia wrangled her long to-do list. The work helped to distract her from the dead mouse and the creepy note. By the time they entered the Lonestar Sugar Shop for the last meeting of the day, she was running on fumes. The scent of buttery frosting caused her mouth to water. Olivia hummed in approval and took a deep breath. "I never tire of the smell of cake."

"Who would?" Cole joined her at the front counter. The display held an assortment of cupcakes topped with gorgeous whirls of icing. Larger cakes rested on the lower shelves. Nearby there was a freezer with enticing ice cream flavors. "Every one of these looks delicious. How often do you have a cake tasting?" His lips curved into a grin. "And do we try them alongside the clients?"

"I do several cake tastings a month. And no, we don't get to try the cake along with the clients." She smoothed a hand down her pencil skirt. "Which is far better for my figure. I'd be ten pounds heavier if I indulged every time I was here."

Cole's attention dropped to her feet and then slowly lifted. He said nothing, but based on the look of appreciation buried in those dark eyes, whatever he was thinking was completely unprofessional. Olivia sensed he didn't believe she needed to shy away from eating cake one bit.

A flush rose in her cheeks. It'd been like this all day. Their eyes would meet during a meeting, or he'd hand her a printout from the copier or make a funny comment, and then she'd blush like a schoolgirl with a secret crush. It was utterly humiliating. And baffling. She hadn't felt one ounce of interest for another man since Aaron's death.

Olivia wanted to dismiss this attraction as misplaced gratitude for everything Cole was doing, but that wasn't honest. There'd been a spark between them before Cole saved her life. It'd been easier to ignore, however, when they only saw each other fleetingly. Spending an entire day together—coupled with Cole's brave actions and their conversations—had turned that initial spark into something more.

Olivia tore her gaze from his, glancing down at the tablet in her hand. "We're meeting with Rosie Jackson and Vincent Santiago." The only appropriate way to handle this unwelcome thrum of attraction zipping between them was by focusing on work. "Their wedding is scheduled for May."

Cole hummed. "Rosie Jackson is the youngest daughter of U.S. Senator Kaylee Jackson. Rosie grew up in Serenity, and after graduating from optometrist school, came back to her hometown to open an eye clinic. She seems down to earth, if her social media is any indication. She volunteers at the local animal shelter, enjoys hiking, and time with her friends. Her finances appear in good order. She drives a Honda and lives in a small apartment near the center of town."

Olivia's brows arched. "Wow. You were thorough in your background checks."

"As thorough as I can be without access to official records." His nose wrinkled as if he'd smelled something sour. "Vincent Santiago is the opposite of Rosie. He likes to party. He owns a towing company and is in massive debt. The only good thing I can say is that he doesn't have a criminal record. I can't imagine what Rosie sees in him, let alone why she'd marry him."

"Sometimes opposites attract."

He snorted in derision. "Sure. That's why so many marriages end in divorce."

Before she could answer, the door to the shop opened. David Martinez, Olivia's former assistant, strolled in. His dirty blond hair had recently been trimmed and stuck up in spikes that were meant to look effortless but failed. His jeans were ripped along the knees and his bright orange undershirt matched the flower tips on the loud Hawaiian button-down he'd thrown on top. An earring dangled from his left earlobe.

The casual look was a far cry from the way Olivia normally saw him. As her assistant, he'd always worn business clothes and a discreet earring. This outfit—the bright colors and artistic style—fit his personality much better.

Olivia smiled in greeting. "David! How nice to see you." She gave him a sisterly hug. "What are you doing in town?"

"I was in the neighborhood visiting a friend and thought I'd take cupcakes to my mom. You know she loves red velvet." His bright blue eyes danced over her face. "But I'm so glad I ran into you. The police questioned me the other day. They said you'd been attacked or something. Is everything okay?"

"I'm fine." Guilt plagued her. David was her friend and it bothered her he'd been questioned like a suspect. "I'm sorry if they showed up out of the blue or caused you any trouble. The police don't have many leads."

"I got that feeling as well. They were asking if I knew of someone who'd want to hurt you. Of course I told them no. Everyone I know loves you." David's gaze drifted to Cole and a questioning look came into his eyes.

Olivia quickly introduced the two men. They shook hands. Pleasantries were exchanged, although the air seemed charged with an uncomfortable tension she couldn't quite place. Both Cole and David seemed to be assessing each other, and neither liked what they saw.

The bakery door swung open again and Rosie burst into the shop with a high-dose of energy. "We're late. I know we're late. It's all my fault." She was followed by a much more subdued Vincent, who affectionately watched as Rosie squealed and embraced David in a big hug. "Are you going to join us for the cake tasting?"

David extracted himself, but his broad smile showed he didn't mind the attention. "I'm afraid not. I've got a dinner date with my mom and she'll be furious if I'm late."

Olivia greeted her clients. Then she gestured toward Cole. "Allow me to introduce my new assistant, Cole Donnelly. He'll be joining us for the cake tasting and will work with me on your wedding."

Rosie pumped Cole's hand with excited energy. "Nice to meet you. I'm Rosie." She stepped back and wrapped an arm around Vincent's waist. "This is my fiancé, Vince. We don't share the same taste in cake flavors, so this meeting may not be a great first impression."

"Don't listen to Rosie." Vincent smiled ruefully. "I've already resigned myself to eating vanilla cake, so there won't be a lick of fighting."

Cole chuckled as he shook Vincent's proffered hand. "Pleasure to meet you."

"The table is set for the tasting." Olivia gestured toward a room in the back of the bakery. "The baker will run through the flavors. I'll join you in just a moment."

The happy couple moved in that direction, Rosie's giggles traveling as Vincent tickled her waist before they entered the back room.

David shook his head. "They're funny."

Olivia agreed. She liked the couple and thought they were a good balance for each other. Different didn't always mean bad. "Speaking of couples, how are you and Angie?" David had quit his job and moved to Houston in order to be closer to his fiancé. "Have you set a date for the wedding yet?" She grinned. "I know a good wedding planner."

David's expression faltered as his gaze skittered from hers. "Angie and I are going through a rough patch. I don't really want to talk about it." He shifted in his high-top sneakers. "The move to Houston was supposed to help our relationship. I think it just made the cracks bigger."

"I'm sorry to hear that." Olivia kicked herself for asking in front of Cole. He'd drifted away and was engrossed in a text message on his phone, but she sensed it was all for show. He was hanging on every word. And David was a private person.

She placed a hand on his arm. "If you ever want to talk, I'm a phone call away."

"Thanks." David smiled and then gave her a bear hug, nearly lifting Olivia off her feet.

The unexpected embrace caught her off-guard. They'd hugged in the past, but the affection had been sibling-like. This was far more intimate. His arm was like a vise around her waist, her chest pushed against his. His other hand played with the long strands of her hair. It made her uncomfortable, and she pushed against his chest to wriggle free. David immediately released her.

Cole appeared at her side. She stepped back, putting some distance between herself and David, nearly tripping on her high heels in the process. Nerves gathered in her stomach. She had the urge to flee. Her mind flashed back to the night of the attack. The assailant's arm around her waist, holding her in place. A sour taste filled her mouth.

Cole put himself between Olivia and David. Either he'd sensed her distress or he hadn't liked the hug. She couldn't tell, but was grateful for the protective move.

David extended a hand toward Cole. "Nice to meet you, man. Make sure you take care of Olivia. She pours a lot of herself into her clients and is a perfectionist, which can make her demanding to work for." David's gaze drifted toward Olivia. Warmth and affection shone in his expression. "But there's no one better."

She blinked. The flashback faded, leaving her weak-kneed. She was being ridiculous. David was her friend. Still, Olivia couldn't shake the need to put some distance between them. "We should go, Cole. Vincent and Rosie are waiting for us." She nodded toward David, forcing a smile on her lips. "It was nice to see you. All the best to your mom."

"Thanks."

Olivia turned and headed for the tasting room.

Cole caught up to her with long strides. "You okay?"

His voice was pitched low enough only she could hear it. Olivia nodded slightly in response. She was fine. Or as fine as she could be. Cole didn't say anything more, but she knew he'd observed the entire interaction with a lawman's perspective. Doubts caused her to second-guess her initial rejection of David as a suspect. But that was silly, right? He had an alibi for the night she was attacked.

Still, no amount of mental reassurance removed the knot in the center of her stomach.

That hug had been... wrong somehow.

Olivia glanced over her shoulder. David stood in the center of the bakery, hands in his pockets, watching her.

Their gazes met.

And something in his expression made her blood run cold.

ELEVEN

The interaction with David at the bakery haunted Olivia. She tried to put it out of her mind during dinner with her grandparents, but it was a struggle. Every interaction between her and David over the last year replayed like a movie. She analyzed them with a new perspective, wondering if she'd been ignorant to her assistant's hidden feelings and motives.

"Are you okay, dear?"

An age-spotted hand covered Olivia's. She glanced up to find her grandmother gazing at her, worry pinching her mouth and deepening the wrinkles along her forehead. Alyssa Leighton was nearly eighty-six, and while time had softened the stunning good looks of her youth, it hadn't robbed her of the innate kindness that was the hallmark of her personality. Everyone in town knew that if you had a problem, Alyssa was the person to talk to. Wise, affectionate, and trustworthy, she'd been one of the most celebrated teachers in Serenity before her retirement.

Olivia forced a smile to ease her grandmother's concern. "I'm alright, Granny. Just lost in thought."

"And it's not a wonder with what you've been dealing with." Willie Leighton, Olivia's grandfather, slammed his water glass down on the table. Indignation heated his ruddy cheeks. His close-cropped hair was thinning, leaving him with a high forehead that accented his sky-blue eyes. They were the same shade as Olivia's. She'd inherited her grandfather's coloring, along with his strong will. Willie was a fighter. Literally. He'd been a prize-winning boxer. Right now, he looked angry enough to punch someone. "I'm gonna have a word with Chief Sims first thing in the morning. This stalker nonsense has to stop."

"Grandpa, the police are doing everything they can. Yelling at Chief Sims won't help. It'll only raise your blood pressure and the doctor specifically said you need to stay calm."

He glowered. "Calm, my foot. How on earth can I stay calm when my only grandchild is attacked while walking to her car?" Willie turned his dark gaze on her. "And when this is all said and done, you and I are going to have a talk, young lady. You should've called us right after the incident happened."

"Willie Gene Leighton, don't you dare lecture Olivia." Alyssa's tone brooked no argument. "She's a grown woman and can share what she wants with us."

He grunted. "That may be, but we're a family. We watch out for each other."

Guilt prickled Olivia. She shot her grandfather an apologetic glance. "I'm sorry for not calling you last night. I didn't want to ruin the last day of your vacation."

"Well, you should have." His tone was gruff, but there was no anger behind it. "Nothing is more important than you."

Shoot. Tears pricked her eyes, and she leaned over to kiss his weathered cheek. "I'm sorry. I didn't mean to upset you. That's the last thing I want." She squeezed her grandmother's hand. "I don't want either of you to worry. Chief Sims is doing everything he can to find my attacker. In the meantime, Cole is keeping an eye on me. I can't get into too much trouble with a Texas Ranger following my every move."

As if her words had called him, there was a knock on the back door. Olivia got up to answer it. Cole greeted her with a smile, and when he crossed over the threshold, the scent of his cologne—something warm and peppery—tingled her senses.

He toed off his boots, nose lifting in the air like a bloodhound. "What is that delicious smell?"

"My grandmother's famous bourbon chicken. I hope you brought your appetite because she made plenty."

"I don't want to be a burden—"

"Nonsense. Granny loves to feed people." She grabbed his hand and gently pulled him from the mudroom into the kitchen. Cole had met her grandparents earlier in the evening, so no introductions were necessary. "Granny, Cole's here. And he's hungry."

Alyssa jumped from her chair with a huge smile. "I'm so glad you could join us, Cole. Please, sit down. I'll fix you a plate. You don't have any allergies, do you? I've made bourbon chicken, sweet potatoes, collard greens, and biscuits. There's also cherry cobbler for dessert."

"No, ma'am. No allergies. Everything sounds wonderful." He claimed the chair next to Olivia. "Ya'll don't eat like this every night, do you? If so, I won't be able to stay for too long." Cole patted his flat stomach. "I'll get fat and spoiled."

Willie grinned at him. "No one's cookin' is better than my Alyssa's." He sat back in his chair and rubbed his ample stomach. "And yes, you'll definitely get fat and spoiled if you stick around. Not that anyone here will complain. As far as I'm concerned, you're a hero. What you've done for our Olivia... we'll never be able to repay you."

"Thank you, sir." Cole glanced at Olivia, his expression warm, as she set a glass of water on his placemat. Then he focused back on the older man. "But there's no need to repay me. I'm glad I was in the right place at the right time."

"Still, you'll always have a place at our table." Alyssa sat a full plate of food in front of Cole.

He bowed his head and said grace before picking up his fork. "This looks delicious. I haven't had a home cooked meal in a good long while."

The conversation was lighthearted as they all ate.

Olivia's grandparents shared old stories about the town. Cole talked about his grandmother. It was clear from the wistful way he spoke about his Nana that he missed her a great deal. Sometime during dessert, Alyssa began showing photographs of Olivia as a child.

She groaned and covered her face when they got to a particularly disastrous junior high picture. Her permed hair stuck out in all directions and her teeth were encased in braces. "Granny, put that away." Olivia reached for the album. "I'm burning that one."

"Don't you dare." Cole's eyes twinkled with amusement. "It's adorable. Tell me, what do you call that hairstyle?"

Olivia lightly punched his shoulder. The muscles underneath were firm. "It was very popular at the time, I'll have you know." She huffed as her cheeks heated. "It just didn't age well."

"The hairstyle might not have, but you did."

Cole's offhand comment warmed her straight through. Before she could think much about it, though, Alyssa was flipping to a new picture. This time of the entire family. Cole studied it and smiled. "You look like both of your parents, Olivia. You've got your dad's eyes and mouth, but your mother's forehead and cheeks."

Alyssa beamed. "She's the best version of all of us."

"That she is." Willie thumped the table in agreement. Then he checked his watch. "Alyssa, it's nearly time for our show. Why don't we leave these two to finish up their desserts while we watch TV for a bit? The dishes can wait."

They went into the living room. Moments later, voices from the television filtered into the kitchen. Cole tilted his head. "What are they watching?"

"Matlock. I've shown Grandpa how to record it several times, but he never remembers to do it. Secretly, I think they like watching it, commercials and all. Reminds them of how things used to be."

Cole chuckled. "They're great. You have a nice family, Olivia."

"Thanks. I think so." She wiped the last crumbs off her mouth with a napkin and leaned back in her chair. "I ate too much. Remind me not to skip lunch again. I turn into a ravenous monster at dinnertime if I do."

She rose from her chair and started clearing the table. Cole got up to help her, but she waved him down. "You're a guest." Her mouth quirked. "And a hero. I'll get a stern talking to if Granny comes in here and sees you doing the dishes."

"Nonsense. I'm practically a member of the family." He winked. "Your grandpa said so."

Olivia laughed. Together, they cleared the table, and she filled the right side of the sink with soapy water. There was no dishwasher. Her grandmother insisted on doing them the old-fashioned way. Cole retrieved a towel from the nearby countertop. They settled into an easy routine, with Olivia washing and Cole drying. It felt intimate and yet comfortable at the same time.

As much as Olivia wanted to stay in this peaceful place, the incident with David wouldn't stop plaguing her. She scrubbed a glass. "When the Houston Police

Department talked to David, they verified he had an alibi for the night I was attacked, right?"

"He was supposedly with his mom. However, they could both be lying."

That wasn't what she wanted to hear. Olivia bit her lip. "The way he hugged me in the bakery today... it was the first time he's ever done that. I keep thinking about our interactions over the year he worked for me, wondering if I missed something. Like maybe he had feelings for me and I never knew it. And then my mind spins in a circle because I could be misconstruing innocent encounters—"

"I don't think you're misconstruing anything." Cole stepped closer and gently removed the glass from her hands. "That's clean. If you scrub it anymore, it'll turn into sand."

She blew out a breath, sending a strand of hair fluttering across her forehead. Then she turned to face him. "So you still think David could be my stalker?"

"I think it's a possibility. He was polite when you introduced me as your assistant, but there was an undercurrent of jealousy. David was being territorial. I think that's what the hug was about." Rather than an I-told-you-so tone, Cole's voice was filled with sympathy. "While we were at the bakery, I texted Eli and asked him to do a deeper background check on David. He called right before dinner. David was arrested in college for stalking his ex-girlfriend. The charges were dropped. But still..."

"If he did it once, he could do it again." Olivia

planted her palms on the counter. She was sick to her stomach.

She felt rather than saw Cole come closer. A moment later, his firm and gentle hand cupped her nape. His fingers slid between the strands of her hair. Unlike when David touched her, Olivia felt no urge to pull away. In fact, it was the exact opposite. She was tempted to turn and bury her head in his broad chest.

"It's going to be okay, Olivia. Eli is currently looking for David's ex-girlfriend. In a day or two, we'll have more answers."

"I don't want this to be someone I know. Someone I trust."

"I know."

His voice was full of so much sympathy, it nearly cracked her. Olivia was used to relying on herself. Had been doing it for a long time. She had her grandparents, yes, but rarely leaned on them. They worried too much about her as it was. She didn't want to make it worse. And Aaron... he'd been wonderful, but he'd always tried to fix the issue. He'd never simply supported her through it.

She was so tired. Being strong every hour of every day was exhausting. And just once she wanted to fall apart and know it was okay.

Cole came closer. With a gentle tug, he pulled her into his arms. "I know you're scared, but I've got you, Olivia. You're not alone."

Those kind words, coupled with his gentle embrace, unleashed her tears. She stopped fighting them, instead wrapping her arms around Cole's waist and giving into her desire to rest her head on his chest. His steady heartbeat thumped against her ear. He was warm. Solid. Strong and brave. Everything she needed to get through this.

A loud blaring from her cell phone interrupted the moment. Olivia jolted. She stepped out of the sanctuary of Cole's arms and crossed the kitchen. An alert flashed on her screen.

"What is it?" Cole asked.

Any sense of safety fled, leaving nothing but fear in its place. "It's an alert from my new security system. Someone's in my house."

TWELVE

Cole removed Olivia's cell phone from her white-knuckled grip as quickly as he could without hurting her. Urgency fueled his movements as he accessed the live feed from the cameras on her home. The screen from a rear bedroom window lay on the grass. A curtain panel, pulled through the broken pane by the wind, fluttered like a flag. Someone was inside the house.

The stalker. He obviously wasn't aware that Olivia was staying with her grandparents across the street. Sienna had made good on her word, and a new security system was installed in Olivia's house this afternoon. It included the ability to control lights inside the house remotely. Cole had programmed it to turn on and off lamps in the living room and primary bedroom throughout the evening.

Additionally, the alarm, when tripped, was also silent, thanks to a programmable setting. The intruder didn't know the security system had sent an alert to

Olivia's phone. As far as he was concerned, no one knew about his presence inside the house.

Keeping an eye on the cameras, Cole used his own phone to call the Serenity Police Department. He quickly identified himself and reported the intruder. Officers were en route, but it would take them fifteen minutes to get there. Far too long. Frustration twisted Cole's insides.

What would the stalker do once he realized Olivia wasn't home? Would he come across the street to her grandparents? It was a possibility. The stalker hadn't attempted to hurt anyone other than Olivia, but that was small comfort. As his desperation grew, so would the potential of harm to innocent bystanders.

First things first, he needed to take precautions. Cole gently snagged Olivia's arm. "Let's go."

He pulled her from the kitchen into the living room.

Willie sat up in his recliner, sensing trouble. "What's the matter?"

"Someone broke into Olivia's house. I need the three of you inside the primary bedroom closet. Now." Cole had planned for every contingency. The closet was an interior room with one way in and out. If the stalker decided to make his way across the street, he'd have to go through Cole in order to get to Olivia and her family.

Willie helped Alyssa from her own recliner before hustling to the hall closet. He pulled a hard-sided case from the top shelf and quickly opened it, revealing a shotgun. The weapon was so clean it practically sparkled. Willie efficiently loaded the weapon. Determination glinted in his steely gaze. "No one is touching my girls. What do you need, Cole?"

He hesitated. He desperately wanted to go after the stalker. To stop this now. But his first priority had to be Olivia. She'd taken her grandmother to the primary bedroom closet. For the moment, the women were safe. Cole checked the security camera on Olivia's cell phone. No change. The intruder was still inside.

Hunting for his prey? Or did he have another plan in mind?

"Officers are fifteen minutes out." Cole pulled his own weapon from its holster. "The stalker doesn't know he tripped the alarm. Once he figures out Olivia isn't there, he could leave. Or he may come here."

"Either way, the best thing to do is take the fight to him." Willie jerked his chin. "Go. I've got my family covered."

Cole didn't need any further encouragement. Willie was armed and capable. He'd do what was necessary to keep his wife and granddaughter safe. The sooner Cole caught the culprit, the better for everyone. He marched to the front door. "Lock this. And set the alarm."

"Done." Willie grabbed the door. "Stay safe, son."

The blessing was said like a prayer. Cole slipped out onto the porch and waited for Willie to secure the house before he ran across the street. Darkness encased him. Thunder rumbled in the distance. A storm was brewing. It kicked up the wind, shaking leaves from the trees. The cold slid down Cole's shirt collar. Goosebumps rose on his arms. He hadn't grabbed a jacket before stepping outside.

Sticking to the shadows, Cole approached the side of Olivia's house. There was a sliding glass door leading to the dining room. Curtains blocked his view of the interior. But this entrance was the safest and easiest way into the house. The new security system allowed it to be opened with a fingerprint. Cole's was already programmed in. He pressed his thump to the pad, and the light changed from red to green.

Lord, be with me. Give me the strength and ability to catch Olivia's stalker.

The glass door slid open silently. Cole's pulse jumped as he used a finger to shift the curtain enough to see inside the room.

Empty. A floor lamp illuminated the space. There was no sign of the intruder. Cole entered the house, weapon leading the way. His gaze swung into the kitchen. Also empty. Nothing appeared disturbed.

He paused, listening for any unusual sound. Warm air blew from the vents in the ceiling. His pulse threatened to gallop out of control, but Cole took a deep breath to counteract the adrenaline racing through his veins. He loosened the grip on his weapon to keep his muscles from freezing up.

Using the wall as protection, he approached the hallway. It was dark. Three doors jutted off. One was a guest bedroom turned into a home office. The other was a bathroom. The last room at the end of the hall was the primary bedroom. Entering without clearing each room was potentially deadly. There was no way to know where the intruder was.

Cole hesitated. He wanted to catch Olivia's stalker with every cell in his body, but he'd already bucked against his training by entering the house alone. The smart thing to do was retreat and wait for the Serenity police officers. But they were still ten minutes out. And likely were responding with lights and sirens on. The minute the intruder heard them, he'd take off.

No. Catching this guy was the priority.

There. A scraping sound drifted down the hall from the primary bedroom. Another followed. The intruder was definitely still here. Cole eased down the hallway on silent steps. Olivia's bedroom was dark. A faint glow drifted from around the corner of the doorway, as though the intruder was using a flashlight on his phone.

Gun leading the way, Cole swung into the bedroom. "Freeze!"

The intruder jolted. He was dressed in all black and a ski mask covered his face. He held a cell phone in his mouth, the flashlight pointed toward an open dresser drawer. One hand held jewelry. The other a gun.

Suddenly, the intruder rushed him. Cole dodged a full-body tackle, but couldn't avoid the assailant all together. His leg slammed into the corner of the night-stand and an elbow to the gut knocked the breath from his body. A lamp fell to the floor, crashing to pieces. Pain vibrated through him. Before he could get his bearings, the intruder took off down the hall.

Sucking in a breath, Cole shoved to a standing position. His ribs had been crushed against the wall and the man. They ached as he bolted down the hall in pursuit. "Freeze!"

The man paid him no heed.

As Cole exited the hallway, a bullet whizzed past his ear. It thudded into the wall behind him.

Instinct and training took over as Cole lunged for safety behind the couch. More bullets punched holes above his head. Sheetrock rained down on him. His heart thundered in his ears as he belly-crawled to a better position. He rose up quickly to get a bead on the intruder just in time to see the man slipping out the sliding glass door. Cole followed but stopped in the doorway. His gaze swung right and left. Sirens wailed in the distance. Too little, too late.

The man was gone.

Muttering an uncharacteristic curse, Cole dialed in to dispatch to update the responding officers. He quickly listed a description of the intruder while circling back to the bedroom. Forensics would do a thorough search. Cole didn't want to disturb any evidence, so he used his cell phone flashlight to illuminate the room.

Dresser drawers hung open, clothes leaking out as though they'd been rifled through. Olivia's jewelry box was tipped over. Some of the contents spilled onto the floor. Most of it was missing though. The closet door was cocked open. Shoe boxes had been searched and then discarded. Glass littered the carpet from the broken window.

Confusion knotted Cole's insides. Was this a simple

robbery? Had he been wrong to assume the break-in was connected to the threats against Olivia?

He turned and his heart stuttered. A butcher knife jutted from the center of Olivia's bed.

Cole stepped closer, his anger growing as the words on the note secured by the blade were revealed by his flashlight.

Get rid of your new assistant. I don't like him. He's not right for you and seeing him with you makes me angry.

Don't disobey me, sweet Olivia.

If you do, he'll pay the ultimate price.

THIRTEEN

Olivia wrapped the ends of her sweater tighter around her midsection to ward off the chill that'd settled in her bones. Her house was a crime scene. Police cars lined the street. Officers and forensic technicians traipsed in and out her front door. A steady rain kept most of the neighbors on their porches. Chief Sims stood under an umbrella, speaking with a news crew.

She watched it all unfold from the safety of her grandparents' living room. The fireplace was on, the heat spilling into the room, warming every inch. But it wasn't enough. Goosebumps pebbled her skin and her fingers trembled. As horrible as the scene before her was, it could've been far worse. The intruder had shot at Cole. He could've been killed. A horrifying proposition.

"Okay, I've got the video cued up." Eli's voice cut through Olivia's thoughts.

She turned. Eli stood next to the bookshelves with the television remote in his hand. He'd logged into the security system at her house to review the footage. Parked in her grandfather's recliner was Texas Ranger Jackson Barker. He'd shed his sports coat and rolled up the sleeves of his white button-down. A five-o'clock shadow riding his jawline darkened at the cleft in his chin. His green eyes and chiseled features were striking paired with his curly hair and tawny skin, but Olivia hadn't felt so much as a blip when they were introduced months ago during a tux fitting for Eli's wedding.

Her gaze flitted to Cole. He lounged on the couch, long legs stretched out in front of him. Sheetrock dust coated sections of his dark hair. He also sported a five-o'clock shadow, the whiskers accenting the masculine curve of his lips. Looking at him now, no one would suspect he'd been involved in a firefight an hour ago with a gunman.

Her pulse picked up speed when Cole's gaze lifted. He patted the cushion next to him in silent invitation. Olivia crossed the room. She claimed the seat, and Cole scooted closer until their shoulders were touching. The heat from his body seemed to sink right through the sleeve of her sweater. She stopped trembling.

"Everyone ready? Here we go." Eli hit play on the remote. On the television screen, a man dressed in all black entered the front yard. "He approached from the neighbors. Probably parked a few streets over. He jumps Olivia's fence and circles around to the backyard."

Olivia watched the man remove the screen from her bedroom window. She shuddered. Normally, at that time, she'd be in bed sleeping. What would've happened if she'd been there?

Cole took her hand. His touch was gentle, but also strong. A silent reminder that she was okay and so was he. His words from earlier in the evening had touched her deeply. *You aren't alone.* Even after being threatened and shot at, Cole was sticking by her side. Comforting her. It unleashed a longing inside her, a hidden desire to be loved and cherished and protected. To share her life with someone who stood by her. Olivia thought those feelings died with Aaron. Or at least, they'd been put on ice. But Cole's steadfast presence had unlocked them, and she didn't have the emotional wherewithal to fight against it.

She interlaced their fingers and focused on the surveillance footage. The intruder used the butt of his gun to break the window. Then he crawled into her bedroom.

Eli paused the video and turned to her. "I know it's hard to tell because the intruder sticks to the shadows, but does anything about him seem familiar?"

She frowned. "Can you play the video again?" Eli did as she requested, and Olivia paid close attention to the intruder's gait and movements. "Something about him is familiar, but... I can't say for certain why." Her gaze bounced to each of the Texas Rangers. "Do you think this is David?"

"David swears he was with his mother all evening." Jackson leaned forward in the recliner, elbows resting on his knees. "The mother confirmed it when officers interviewed her. However, a neighbor said they observed

David's car driving up the street at nine o'clock. If the neighbor is telling the truth—and there's no reason to think he's lying—then David wasn't at his mom's house at the time of the break-in."

Olivia blew out a breath. "That's not good."

She didn't like believing her former assistant had anything to do with stalking her, but ignoring the facts in front of her would be foolish. "The intruder is about the right height and weight, but nothing about the way he moves reminds me of David." She struggled to put into words the reason why. Eli kept the video playing on a loop. "It's the gait. David is long-legged and bounces when he walks. This guy is more contained in his movements."

"Could be nerves," Eli observed. "Or we're barking up the wrong tree. I don't think it's a good idea to narrow our suspect list to David. I spoke to his ex-girlfriend from college. The one he was accused of stalking. According to her, David showed up at her dorm begging for a second chance after they broke up. He did this for days until finally the campus police encouraged her to take out a restraining order. Once she did, David stopped bothering her. As far as I can tell, he's stayed out of trouble since."

"Have you spoken to his current girlfriend, Angie?" Olivia asked.

Jackson waved a finger. "I did. She said David is a great guy. He's never been violent, although she admitted that he has a temper and is prone to jealousy. That's a big issue they're dealing with right now. He doesn't like one of the guys at her job. Angie believes that's a ridiculous complaint, especially since—and this is a direct quote—David is infatuated with you. It's the reason Angie insisted he quit and move back to Houston."

"Infatuated?" Olivia released Cole's hand and rose from the couch to pace. The anxiety inside her was building, and she needed to release it somehow. "That's extreme. A crush perhaps, but... I can't believe I would miss an infatuation."

"You've been grieving." Cole's voice was nonjudgmental. "Dating wasn't even on your radar until recently. It's possible you never noticed how David felt about you because your focus was somewhere else."

She had to admit he had a point. She halted mid-step. "So what? The encounter with David in the cake shop was a setup? He came in under the guise of buying cupcakes so he could figure out who I was with."

Cole shrugged. "It's possible. He was giving off territorial vibes when you introduced us. Like I said, I think that's what the hug was about. He was putting me on notice."

"It would explain the stalker's threat tonight," Jackson added. "He doesn't like seeing you with Olivia. He's jealous."

"There is one thing that bothers me about tonight's break-in though." Cole leaned forward. "If the goal was to threaten me and scare Olivia, why did he rifle through her things and steal her jewelry?"

"Opportunity."

Cole shook his head. "This wasn't the first time he'd broken into her house. He did it last night and didn't steal anything. What changed?" He squinted at the television screen. "It makes me wonder if there's more than one person involved. As though the person who broke in tonight and the one who broke in yesterday aren't the same."

Olivia's stomach clenched. "That doesn't make any sense. If the stalker is infatuated with me, then why would he have someone else break into my house?"

"To avoid getting caught." Cole shrugged. "Whoever's behind this has been incredibly careful. Today, he was sloppy. He tripped the alarm and didn't notice, then took time to rifle through your belongings after leaving the note and knife in your bed. It's possible he's escalating and just getting careless, but this seemed out of character from his previous attacks."

Olivia rubbed her head. A headache was brewing along her temples. It was terrifying having one man after her. She didn't want to consider that her stalker had hired someone else to do his dirty work. "I want to talk to Susan. She worked with David just as much as I did. If he's infatuated with me, as Angie claims, then I guarantee Susan noticed. Truthfully, I should've told her about the stalking earlier." She dropped her hand and gestured to the window where a news crew filmed the front of her house. "Chief Sims wanted to keep the attacks against me quiet, but that's no longer possible."

"I agree." Eli clicked the television off. "Cole, your cover is still in place, so I think you should continue working as her assistant. Like I said, I don't want to limit our investigation to David. If the stalker hired someone to break into Olivia's house, then he's keeping his distance. It gives us time to find him before he can plan his next move."

Olivia chewed on her bottom lip. She didn't want Cole getting hurt in the process of protecting her. "As much as I hate to admit it, maybe Cole was right and I should lie low. I have a wedding this weekend that I need to see through, but after that, I can move some commitments around."

Cole shook his head. "We don't have to decide that right now."

"But the stalker threatened you—"

"It'll take a lot more than a silly note and some bullets to scare me off." He met her gaze, his jaw set and determined. "I'm in this, Olivia, and I'm not going anywhere until it's finished."

FOURTEEN

The scent of fresh coffee greeted Cole as he followed Olivia into Blessed Events. He breathed in deep. He'd already had two cups this morning with breakfast, but the caffeine had done little to ward off the exhaustion weighing him down. Months of working murder cases prior to taking on the role as Olivia's bodyguard had left him sleep deprived.

Susan wasn't behind her desk. A note stated she was running a quick errand and would be back soon. Cole beelined for the kitchen and poured two mugs of coffee. After adding hazelnut creamer to Olivia's, he brought it to her office. Her laptop was powering on. She wore slacks and a soft burgundy suit jacket that made the caramel highlights in her hair even more noticeable. Makeup framed her gorgeous eyes, but couldn't completely erase the dark circles underneath them. She hadn't slept well last night either. Or the night before. The amount of stress and pressure she'd been under for the last several weeks tugged at Cole's emotions. He wanted to shift some of those burdens off her delicate shoulders.

"Here." He handed her the mug of coffee. "It's creamer with a touch of caffeine."

Olivia laughed. The sound reminded Cole of the wind chimes on his grandmother's back porch.

She took the cup from him. "Hazelnut makes everything better. Coffee. Chocolate. Ice cream. I even have a recipe for a creamy pumpkin pasta sauce with hazelnuts that will knock your socks off."

His nose wrinkled. Hazelnuts were okay, but paired with pumpkin?

"I might be able to get behind the hazelnut ice cream, but in my pasta... that's a step too far." Cole sipped his own black coffee. "Still, I'm man enough to try it. Convince me otherwise."

She arched a pretty brow, a smile quirking her lips. "Challenge accepted."

They shared a laugh. Then Cole gestured to the mood board propped up behind her desk. "The Gonzales wedding is tomorrow. Are you ready?"

"I think so. After we talk to Susan, I'd like to pop over to the Oak Gardens and inspect the ballroom. Make sure everything is going according to plan."

Cole nodded. He'd already researched the venue's layout. It was a local establishment with gorgeous outside gardens, a small chapel, a ballroom for formal weddings, and a rustic barn for more casual receptions.

Eli and Sienna had rented Oak Gardens for their

wedding as well. They would get married in the small chapel and have their reception in the barn. Cole could barely process that he needed his speech ready by next weekend. What was he going to say? He didn't like public speaking, but that wasn't what worried him the most. It was the topic. How could he give a speech worthy of his friends without allowing any of his own negative feelings about marriage to seep in?

The memory of the car crash that'd taken his parents' lives replayed in his mind. Harsh words and yelling. The accusations of cheating. Cole, his voice cracking with pain and frustration, screaming at his parents to stop from the back seat. Then the crash of metal and the sound of shattering glass that followed.

Cole had survived. His parents hadn't. And to this day, he blamed himself for distracting his dad by screaming. It'd caused the accident.

"Earth to Cole." Olivia waved a hand in front of his face. "Are you okay? You were lost in thought."

He blinked, as the memory faded, leaving him hollowed out. "Sorry, I was thinking about my speech for Eli's wedding." Cole swallowed hard as the urge to tell Olivia about his past took root. He rarely discussed it, even with Nana, but something about Olivia's loving nature made him want to open up. "I'm honored Eli asked me to be a part of the wedding, but I'm the last person on earth who should give a speech about love and marriage."

"Why is that?"

Before Cole could answer, the bells over the entrance

jingled. Susan strolled in. She'd wrangled her curls into a ponytail and carried a bag from the local pharmacy.

She beelined right for Olivia and embraced her in a hug. "I'm so glad you're okay. The break-in at your house was all over the news this morning. Everyone in town is talking about it."

Cole grimaced. He'd debated the wisdom of telling Susan about Olivia's stalker, but ultimately decided she was right. The woman was a busybody, but she was also observant. Her perspective on the interactions between David and Olivia might prove valuable.

"Thank you for calling me this morning." Olivia extracted herself from Susan's embrace. "And for handling phone calls from worried clients."

"Of course." Susan hurried back to the front desk, her voice trailing behind her. "Sorry about not being here when you arrived. My husband is having back trouble and demanded I get him some disposable heat packs." She tossed the bag on a chair and shed her coat. "Men. God forbid Mitch get his own things from the pharmacy."

Olivia grimaced at Susan's caustic tone. "Has he seen a doctor about his back?"

"Of course." Susan sighed with annoyance. "The doctor thinks Mitch strained his back on a construction site. They told him to take a few weeks off. My husband is currently lying around at home with his feet up watching football day and night."

"It must be serious if the doctor thinks he needs rest," Cole said. It also explained why Mitch asked Susan to pick up the items from the pharmacy. The shop was five stores down from Blessed Events. "I hope he feels better soon."

"Me too. We have bills to pay, and I don't want to be the only one responsible for them." Susan returned to Olivia's office with a stack of messages in her hands. "These are the most important ones. Randy, the head chef at Oak Gardens, needs to speak to you about the Gonzales wedding. The florist also wanted to know if you're stopping by this afternoon to see the venue."

"I am. I can talk to Randy then too." Olivia took the messages from her secretary. She flipped through them and a lottery ticket dropped out.

Susan scooped it up, a blush rising in her cheeks. "Oops. Sorry about that. It must've gotten mixed in by mistake."

"I thought you'd stopped playing the lottery."

She shrugged in reply. "Do the police have any idea who broke into your house?" Susan's expression was one of concern, but it was clear from the gleam in her eye that she was interested in extracting as much information about the case as possible. "I know something serious has been going on for a while, but I became very concerned when Chief Sims was mysteriously in our offices the other day. You've been jumpy for weeks."

Olivia gestured to the chair in front of her desk. "I'm sorry, Susan. There is something going on, but the chief specifically asked me to keep it quiet so he could fully investigate."

Susan's mouth flattened into a thin line. "And you didn't think you could trust me with the truth?"

Hurt layered her voice, but Cole suspected she was more insulted than betrayed by Olivia's lack of confidence. Susan might be an excellent secretary, but she wasn't someone to confide in. Not if Olivia didn't want her news plastered all over town.

Cole had spent most of the day yesterday with Susan. He'd probed her about various clients and she'd told him everything from their shoe size to family feuds. Most of the information was harmless, but some of it was downright nasty. Cole fully understood why the chief wanted to keep Susan out of the loop.

Regret and shame flooded Olivia's expression. She clearly hated that she'd hurt the other woman's feelings. "I'm sorry. It wasn't my decision." She folded her hands over her desk. "But circumstances have changed with the break-in. I've been receiving threatening notes for weeks from a stalker."

Olivia explained everything, from the messages to the attacks.

Susan listened without saying a word, her brow furrowed with what appeared to be concern. "And Chief Sims believes the person who broke into your house last night is the same one who's stalking you?"

"Yes. The police believe David might be involved."

Susan's mouth dropped open. She blinked. "David?"

Her shock seemed genuine. Cole had asked Susan about David yesterday, and while she'd been eager to discuss clients, she'd been unusually tight-lipped about

Olivia's former assistant. He'd found it strange at the time. Cole leaned forward. "That surprises you?"

"It's no secret I'm not a fan of David, but I find it hard to believe he's capable of stalking someone. At least... not without getting caught."

"What do you mean?"

"He's flighty and disorganized. David was personable and had an artistic eye, but he was constantly dropping the ball on important matters. Schedules, returning phone calls, budgets. Whatever caught his attention is what he focused on, regardless of what the priorities were. He needed constant reminders to stay on track. I found him utterly exhausting and too high maintenance."

Cole considered Susan's observations. The stalker was controlled and measured. It didn't sound like David was either of those things.

Eli's warning rang in his head. It would be silly to limit their investigation on one man. "Can you think of anyone who might be infatuated with Olivia?"

"Infatuated...." Susan considered it for several heartbeats. "Actually, there is someone."

"Who?"

"The head chef at Oak Gardens."

Olivia's mouth dropped open. "Randy Higgins is married!"

"Actually, he and his wife separated. About six months ago, he was asking about you, specifically whether you were dating anyone." Susan tilted her head. "I considered saying something a while ago, but you've been so negative about dating, I figured there was no point."

Cole needed to tread carefully here. Showing an interest in Olivia was a far cry from stalking her. "What makes you think Randy is infatuated with Olivia? It sounds like he was simply trying to figure out if she was single."

"That's what I thought at first too, but then I caught him watching Olivia in secret while she was at Oak Gardens. He'd hide behind pillars so no one would notice, and couldn't take his eyes off her."

Olivia gaped. "Why didn't you say anything before now?"

Susan cast a derisive glance in her direction. "It seemed harmless at the time. Randy's always been an odd duck. Besides, I didn't know you were being stalked." Her lips flattened into a thin line as she leveled her gaze at Cole. "If you're looking for a suspect, I'd question Randy."

FIFTEEN

Oak Gardens was a beautiful wedding venue situated on several acres of rolling hills. Oak and pecan trees dotted the landscape, providing the perfect backdrop for photographs of the bride and groom. A small lake, with a fountain shooting out of the center, glittered in the sunshine. Entering the arched gates normally brought a smile to Olivia's face. Today, it only made the ball of nerves tighten in her stomach. She regretted having a second cup of coffee this morning. The caffeine didn't help her anxiety.

Cole was stretched out in the passenger seat. He'd spent most of the drive over doing a background check on Randy Higgins. His brow was furrowed as he flipped through documents on his phone.

The anticipation was killing Olivia. She gripped the steering wheel. "Did you find anything interesting?"

"Nope. Randy Higgins, 35, head chef at Oak Gardens. Before that he worked for several restaurants in

Austin. He married his wife five years ago. They don't have any children. Randy isn't very active on social media. It seems he's a private person. Most of his posts are about fishing or hunting." Cole clicked a button to lock his phone. "He's mentioned in a few articles about Oak Gardens. Everyone agrees he's a talented chef."

"He is." Olivia admired the creative way he adapted the menu for each couple. It was one of the reasons she recommended Oak Gardens to clients.

Cole slanted a glance in her direction. "How would you describe your relationship with Randy?"

"Friendly. Respectful." She sighed. "Honestly, I'm shocked by Susan's comments. If Randy was watching me from behind pillars..." Olivia grimaced. "That's creepy."

Before today, she'd never felt uncomfortable for a second in Randy's presence. Nor had she picked up on any romantic interest from him. Then again, she hadn't noticed David's either. It made her feel uncertain and more than a little stupid. How could she have been so blind?

The main building of Oak Gardens loomed large. It was new, but designed to look like a Southern plantation. Winding roads and signs directed people to the chapel or the barn. Neither was visible from the main building, since both were hidden in the trees.

Cole tapped his knee with an index finger. "I find it strange Susan didn't mention Randy's behavior before today."

Olivia pulled into a parking spot in front of the main

building. Then she turned to face him. "You think she's lying?"

"Lying, no. Exaggerating... perhaps. Susan strikes me as someone who likes drama."

He wasn't wrong. Olivia's mind spun with the possibilities. She didn't know what to believe anymore. "Lord, give me the wisdom to trust Your guidance. Help us uncover the truth."

"Amen." Cole shot her a heart-stopping smile before hopping out of the truck and circling to open her door.

Olivia grabbed her purse. The February air was nippy despite the sunshine. She tucked her hands into the pockets of her coat. "Game plan?"

"Just interact with Randy as you normally would. I'll take care of the rest."

She nodded and started up the walkway with Cole at her side. Some of her nerves settled as he held open the door to the main building for her. Sometime in the last few days, the trust between them had grown. Spending so many hours together had cemented an easy friendship. One Olivia hoped would continue even after this case was solved.

She peeked at Cole out of the corner of her eye as she crossed over the threshold into the lobby. The scent of his aftershave tickled her senses. Olivia's heart skipped a beat. Who was she kidding? There was more than friendship simmering under the surface of their relationship. But now wasn't the time to entertain anything romantic. Not with a stalker lurking somewhere in the shadows.

"I have to stop in the ballroom and check on the

decor, but let's visit Randy first." Olivia turned down a hall, nodding at staff cleaning the carpets as she headed to the rear of the building. She found Randy in his office off the main kitchen. It was a cramped room, just big enough for a rickety desk and a few chairs. The printer whirred.

"You have perfect timing." Randy grinned. A dimple appeared in his left cheek, making the smile boyish and disarming. Unruly, curly brown hair and round cheeks added to the effect. He wore a chef's jacket and dark jeans. Extra pounds around his midsection showed he liked to eat as much as cook. He waved Olivia and Cole into his office. "I'm going over the menu again for tomorrow's reception."

"Susan said you had an issue." Olivia set her purse down in the chair but didn't bother sitting. "Oh, Randy, this is my new assistant, Cole."

"Nice to meet you." Randy offered Cole an equally bright smile and shook his hand. Then he turned his attention back to Olivia. "The bride wanted lamb sliders with crispy fried onions, but my supplier doesn't have the meat. Something about a lamb shortage this year. We can make beef sliders." He grabbed the paper from the printer. "Or I can substitute one of these appetizers instead. I made sure my supplier has the ingredients."

Olivia took a photograph with her phone of the menu options. "I'll message Avery and ask her." She shot off the text. "Let's give her a minute to see if she replies."

"Sounds good." Randy ran a hand through his hair and his smile lessened. "How are you doing, Olivia? I heard about the break-in at your house on the news. Crazy. Stuff like this isn't common in Serenity. Was it just a robbery?"

"The police are still investigating. Thankfully, I wasn't home at the time."

"I'm glad. My house was broken into in Austin. Robbery. They took jewelry and some cash. My computer. I remember my wife, Jessica, was terrified to stay home alone while I was working at night. It's part of the reason we moved out here." He shook his head and grimaced. "I'm worried this incident will set off her PTSD again."

Didn't Susan say Randy and his wife were separated? It didn't sound that way to Olivia. "That's rough. I know of a great therapist if she needs to talk to someone."

"I'll let her know. Thanks."

Cole gestured to a frame on the desk. Randy had his arm wrapped around a dark-haired beauty. Both of them smiled brilliantly at the camera. "Is that your wife?"

"It is." Randy leaned back in his chair and it creaked. "We went to the Grand Canyon recently for our wedding anniversary. Man, that was a nice trip. We camped for three days." His dimple popped out again. "Jessica loves the outdoors as much as I do."

"You're a lucky guy."

"You don't have to tell me twice." His brow crinkled. "Are you married?"

"Naw. I'm gun shy when it comes to walking down the aisle." Cole adjusted his cowboy hat, a sheepish expression on his face. "I like certainty and marriage seems like a gamble, you know?"

Olivia stiffened slightly. Did Cole genuinely feel that way, or was he simply steering the conversation? She couldn't tell. And now wasn't the time to ask. She kept quiet, letting Cole take control. Clearly he was hoping to find out more about Randy and his wife.

Randy rubbed his chin. "Marriage isn't always easy, but there's nothing better than having a teammate by your side." His gaze went to the photograph on his desk. "Jessica and I went through some hard times, but we loved each other too much to give up. I think that's the key sometimes. Don't give up."

Cole shrugged. "Sometimes it's better to give up though. If you're fighting every day and miserable... what's the point?"

Olivia's heart sank. It definitely sounded like Cole was speaking from experience. No wonder he was struggling to write Eli and Sienna's speech. Was he divorced? It would explain so many of his comments over the last few days. Olivia mentally kicked herself for not asking. Some friend she was.

Randy grimaced. "Fighting ain't good. I agree with you there. But that's when you get help. I ain't ashamed to say that Jessica and I worked with our pastor to sort through our differences. We also made friends with some great married couples who really support us. Sometimes, you think you're the only ones with problems, but then you realize everyone has difficulties. It's improved our marriage more than ever." He eyed Cole speculatively.

"For someone so down on marriage, working for a wedding planner is an interesting career choice."

Cole laughed. "Yes, it is."

Olivia's phone beeped with an incoming text from her client. "Avery says the beef sliders are fine."

Randy leaned forward and circled the selection on his paper. "Great. I'll put the order in right now. The ingredients will be delivered tonight and we'll be ready to go."

"Fantastic." Olivia glanced at Cole, who gave her a subtle nod. He'd gotten whatever information he needed. Olivia turned back to Randy. "Thanks for everything. If you have any other issues, call me."

"Will do." Randy waved bye.

Olivia stepped back into the hall. She waited until they were far enough away from Randy's office before whispering, "Well?"

"Either Randy is an excellent actor or he genuinely loves his wife." Cole frowned. "I don't want to mark him off the suspect list, but I find it hard to believe he's your stalker."

Relief unknotted the tension in Olivia's shoulders. It didn't bring them any closer to identifying her stalker, but at least she hadn't misjudged Randy. "I'm glad. I was starting to doubt my own instincts." She wanted to ask Cole about his earlier comments, but this didn't seem like the right time or place. Later. When they were at home. Instead, Olivia smiled brightly. "The ballroom is our last stop. Then we can head home. Granny is making meat-loaf with mashed potatoes for dinner."

Cole's eyes widened with appreciation. "Sounds delicious."

The ballroom was a chaotic mess. Bare tables waited for linens and flowers. Floor-length windows provided a stunning view of the gardens and the lake. An archway of white roses was being built near the dance floor. Olivia chatted with the florist and her crew. Then with the venue manager. Everything was on track for tomorrow night. She double-checked her task list and then closed her tablet with a sigh of happiness. "All done."

Cole grinned as he crossed the dance floor toward her. "Nothing makes you more content than checking things off your to-do list."

She laughed to offset the way her breath hitched. The man was so handsome, it was distracting. Olivia reminded herself that romance wasn't part of their agreement. "That's true. I love having a checklist, and when everything is ticked off, I feel like my day was productive."

A loud creak overhead jolted Olivia's gaze upward. Shock and horror flooded through her as the chandelier suddenly dropped from the ceiling. Hundreds of pounds of crystals headed straight for the center of the dance floor.

For Cole.

It was going to kill him.

SIXTEEN

Everything happened in the span of a heartbeat.

One second Cole was admiring Olivia's gorgeous smile. The next, he was in deadly trouble.

A loud creak alerted Cole to the danger right before the entire chandelier came rushing at his head. He lunged across the dance floor in a desperate bid to outrace certain death. Pain erupted in his shoulder and hip as he collided with the ground. Olivia screamed his name. He didn't have time to register the panic in her voice.

Cole rolled. The world spun. He bounced off the wooden dance floor onto the carpet before slamming into a table with a teeth-chattering jolt. Instinctively, his arms went up to protect his face as the chandelier hit the dance floor. It shattered. Glass shards flew in his direction. Screams echoed. Cole's heart thumped hard against his ribcage. One of those voices sounded like Olivia. Was she hurt?

Fear gripped his insides. He lowered his arms and opened his eyes. The room was in chaos. People had toppled chairs and flowers to get out of the way of the falling chandelier. He sat up, his gaze scanning the room, searching for Olivia. She wasn't visible. His pulse skyrocketed.

Movement behind him caught Cole's attention a moment before Olivia dropped to his side. Her cheeks were flushed, bright blue eyes flooded with concern. She grabbed his hand. "Are you hurt?"

"I'm fine." Cole didn't give a fig about himself. He stood, bringing Olivia with him. His gaze dropped to her heels, climbed over her shapely legs and up her body, searching for any signs of injury. No blood. She appeared unharmed. *Thank you, Lord.*

Only then did he quickly take an assessment of his own injuries. Nothing serious. A few minor cuts and bruises. Cole knew tomorrow he'd be sore, but that was nothing compared to what could have happened.

The chandelier was a heap of wires and shattered crystals in the center of the ballroom. A long wire stretched from the top all the way to the ceiling. Glass crunched under Cole's boots as he shifted his weight to search the room for anyone who was injured. Several people stood along the edges of the ballroom. "Anyone hurt?"

People shook their heads. He took that as confirmation that no one had been seriously injured by the falling chandelier. Cole snagged his cell phone from his pocket and took photos. "Did anyone see what happened?"

"It just fell." Olivia stared at the heap in the center of the dance floor. Anger heated her voice. "You could've been killed!"

"I'm certain that was the plan." He shot off a text to Eli with some of the photographs before drawing closer to get a better look at the busted chandelier. The hum from a motor reached his ears. Most large light fixtures in professional spaces were attached to a pulley system, which allowed them to be raised and lowered with ease for maintenance or cleaning. Where was the control mechanism?

A silver-haired woman burst into the ballroom. Martha Waterford. The owner of Oak Gardens. Olivia had introduced Cole to Martha earlier in the day. The older woman's eyes widened into shocked circles. She gasped. "What happened?"

"That's what I'd like to know." Cole gestured to the wire hanging from the ceiling. "Is the chandelier on a pulley system?"

"It is." Martha's mouth gaped open. "We had it serviced a few days ago. It was fine."

"Where's the control mechanism?"

She pointed to a section of the ballroom draped in black curtains. "Over there. On the wall." Cole headed to inspect it, Martha and Olivia following right behind. The older woman puffed as she struggled to keep up. "But the box is locked. Only certain people have the key."

Cole yanked the drapery aside to reveal the wall. A small box near the door hung open, the key used to open it still hanging from the lock. Martha shoved him aside and reached for the key, but he put up an arm to block her. "Don't touch anything. The police will be here soon, and they'll want to investigate."

"The police..." Martha pressed a hand against her heart. "Someone did this on purpose?"

"It would seem so. Chandeliers like yours have safety mechanisms to prevent them from falling. Someone bypassed all of them."

The older woman blinked and then resolve hardened her expression. "You're right." She pushed off Cole's hand. "I won't touch the key, but I want to see if I can tell who it belongs to." Martha bent at the waist and peered at the silver round disk dangling from the key chain. Her mouth tightened. "This is the key used by our maintenance crew. It's kept in a secure place behind the front desk."

"How many people have access to it?"

She blew out a breath. "The cabinet is locked, but several people have keys. Both of my secretaries, myself, the cleaning crew supervisor, the security manager, our head chef—"

"Randy Higgins has access to this key?" Cole stiffened. The chef had been personable and treated Olivia with the same deference he afforded Cole. But Susan warned there was a darker side to Randy. Cole might have been wrong to remove him from the suspect list so quickly.

Martha's brow furrowed. "Do you have reason to believe Randy has something to do with this?"

Yes. But Cole didn't think it was a good idea to list

the reasons at the moment. Every second counted and soon Martha might refuse to answer his questions to protect her company name. He pointed to the security camera discreetly hung from the corner of the ceiling. "I need to see your security footage."

"I'm afraid that's not possible." Martha blew out a breath. "Our system went down last night. The company has been informed, and they're sending a repair crew this afternoon."

Several police officers entered the ballroom. Martha excused herself and left to speak to them. Cole watched her go, frustration building until he wanted to punch the wall. But that wouldn't get him anywhere. Instead, he took a deep breath and let it out slowly. His anger was a contained beast. The last time he'd let it out, it'd caused the death of his parents. Cole did everything in his power to keep control.

Olivia touched his arm. "The stalker warned me in his letter that you'd get hurt if I didn't fire you. He attempted to make good on that threat."

"Yes. This was a planned attack." Cole envisioned it all in his mind. "He disabled the security system. Then he stole the key and deactivated the chandelier's safety mechanisms sometime before we arrived today. After that, it was a simple matter of lying in wait behind these black curtains until the perfect moment presented itself."

"Randy is the only person I can think of who has access to both the security system and the chandelier's pulley system."

Cole nodded. Yet something about this situation

didn't feel right. He couldn't put his finger on what though. He scanned the area behind the curtains, looking for anything that might lead to the stalker's identity. The carpet was clean. No help.

He ducked behind the curtains and peeked into the room. Perfect visibility. "I didn't even sense someone was back here." Cole mentally berated himself for being so careless. He'd been caught up in watching Olivia, distracted by the way she chewed on her bottom lip while thinking, the soft waves of her hair, and the beautiful curves of her face. All the while a killer watched them from the safety of his hiding place. It was humiliating. More importantly, it'd nearly cost Cole his life.

How could he have let this happen? He wasn't some naïve schoolboy with his first crush. He was a trained law enforcement officer, for crying out loud. "I should've been paying closer attention."

Olivia placed a hand on his arm. The sweet touch sent his cells humming with attention. "You're not omnipotent. No one could expect you to know someone was hiding behind the drapery."

"Baloney. I'm a Texas Ranger. It's my *job* to know these things."

He shook off her comforting hand. Self-loathing coursed through his veins. What if the chandelier hadn't been meant for him? What if it'd been meant for Olivia? The very thought sent a chill racing down his spine. She wouldn't have been able to escape in time. And Cole would've been to blame.

Olivia stepped into his line of sight. She met his gaze.

"You're an excellent Texas Ranger, but again, you're not omnipotent. You can do everything right and still things can go wrong." She arched her brows. "Maybe the person you should point a finger at is me. I insisted on following through on my commitments to my clients. We wouldn't even be here if it wasn't for me."

Cole narrowed his gaze. "You're not responsible for what your stalker does."

"Neither are you." She let those words hang in the air between them for several beats before adding, "God protected everyone in that room, especially you. And I'm grateful."

Olivia reached for him and then hesitated, likely because he'd brushed off her touch moments ago. Cole couldn't stand the flicker of uncertainty flashing in those enchanting blue eyes. He gently grasped her wrist and pulled her into his arms. Olivia sighed as she rested her head against his chest. Her hair tickled the bottom of his chin. Cole took a deep breath. His first since the chandelier fell. The feel of her nestled in his embrace slowed his heart rate and took the edge off his anger.

Somehow, some way, Olivia had gotten under his skin. She'd awakened desires Cole thought he was immune to. And he didn't know how to stop it. Or even if he wanted to.

There was only one thing Cole was certain of. Olivia's stalker wasn't giving up.

And he would kill anyone standing in his way.

SEVENTEEN

Olivia hummed along with the gospel song on the radio as she iced a chocolate cake. The coffee machine gurgled as it brewed and the faint sound of her grandfather's television show filtered in from the living room. A few dirty dishes still littered the kitchen table. Dinner had been a welcome retreat from the hectic and horrifying events of the day. The familiar routine, and cheerful conversation, had eased some of Olivia's stress.

Granny, her hands tucked into yellow gloves, looked up from doing the dishes and smiled. Her eyes crinkled at the corners. "Happiness suits you, baby girl."

Happiness? Olivia paused, spatula loaded with thick icing. Considering everything that was going on, the last thing Olivia should be was joyful. She grimaced. "In about five minutes, a group of Texas Rangers are going to be in this kitchen to discuss my stalking case. It's probably poor form to be singing along with the radio."

"Nonsense. When things are bleak, we need to find

moments of happiness where we can." Granny's gaze turned speculative. "In fact, I wonder if your good mood has anything to do with one particular Texas Ranger."

Her cheeks heated. "Granny..."

"Don't deny it. I've known you since the day you were born."

Olivia glanced at the kitchen doorway. Cole had eaten dinner with them, but had gone outside to do a perimeter check before the rest of the rangers arrived. He wouldn't overhear their conversation. "Admittedly, there's a spark."

Her grandmother gave a dainty snort. "If the electricity company could use the heat between you two for power, no one in Serenity would have to pay their light bill. Has he kissed you yet?"

"Granny!" The flush in Olivia's cheeks spread down her neck. She focused on icing the cake. "No. Of course not. Cole hasn't even hinted at wanting anything more than friendship. I think he's been burned by love in the past. And to be fair, I've had my own heartache."

Granny's expression turned sympathetic. "Aaron would want you to be happy."

"I know." Olivia didn't have guilt about moving on. "It just feels weird to have feelings for someone new. Exciting too. And scary. It's been so long since I was interested in anyone... and I don't know if Cole feels the same way... It's all jumbled together. I forgot what it was like to have butterflies one minute and uncertainty the next." Her nose wrinkled. "Add in the stalker and things are very complicated."

Her grandmother hummed. "I don't think they're that complicated. Take it from me, Cole's interested. That's not the problem. The timing may not be perfect, but God works in mysterious ways. Just be open and see where this leads."

It was good advice. Olivia tossed the spatula into the empty bowl. "I will." The song changed on the radio and she squealed. "I love this one."

Granny's grin widened. "So sing your heart out."

Olivia laughed as her grandmother began crooning off-key. Together, they filled the kitchen with their voices, drowning out the radio. The music made Olivia's heart lighter. She danced between the table and the sink, removing the last of the dirty dishes. On one turn, she caught sight of Cole. She bumped into the island with her hip as embarrassment heated her cheeks.

He leaned against the doorframe, arms crossed over his broad chest, a smile on his lips. When his gaze met hers, his dark eyes sparkled with amusement. "Don't stop on my account. I love a good concert."

She threw a kitchen towel at him. Cole surprised her by catching it with one hand. Then his rich baritone voice mingled with her grandmother's. Granny tugged off her cleaning gloves, laying them on the counter, as Willie entered the kitchen. His wrinkled face split into a grin as Granny extended her hand. The two of them began dancing.

Olivia's heart swelled at the obvious love between her grandparents. Cole joined her at the island, still singing. He wrapped an arm around Olivia's waist. His touch sent a zing of exhilaration through her. She smiled up at him, loving the way their voices melded together in perfect harmony. Together, they serenaded the couple.

When the song was over, Willie kissed Granny. "It's time for bridge, darlin'. You know how Margie gets when we're late."

"I do." Granny untied her apron and hung it next to the fridge. Then she and Willie danced out of the kitchen. Their laughter lingered as they headed for the front door. Their weekly bridge game was something they looked forward to.

"Your grandparents are amazing." Cole dropped his arm from around Olivia's waist, but didn't move away from her. Instead, he turned to look her in the eyes. "How long have they been married?"

"Forty-two years." Olivia's heart beat erratically as Cole's hand rose to brush a strand of hair off her forehead. His fingertips sent a wave of pleasure through her as they traveled along the sensitive skin at her temple before brushing the shell of her ear.

"I can't imagine what that's like." His voice was almost wistful, the longing in his gaze unmistakable as his attention landed on her lips before rising to meet her eyes. "Spending such a long time with someone and still being in love."

Olivia's breath hitched. "Why not?"

His gaze grew distant. "My parents had a rough marriage. There was a lot of fighting and chaos in my household. They must've been in love at some point, but somewhere along the way, all those feelings died. All that was left was anger and vengeance." Cole stiffened slightly, as if he suddenly realized how close in proximity they were to each other. He released her and backed away. "Sorry. I shouldn't have brought that up."

She wasn't sure if Cole was sorry he'd shared something so personal or was simply apologizing for ruining the romantic moment with something serious. Either way, it bothered her. "You don't need to apologize. I'm glad you told me."

Many of the things he'd said over the last few days made sense. The comments about divorce, his conversation with Randy. Olivia knew he'd been burned, but she'd imagined a bad relationship with a girlfriend, not growing up in a household with constant fighting. No wonder he was so leery of marriage.

Olivia couldn't stop herself from stepping forward to close the distance between them. She laid a hand on his chest, right over his heart. Cole's flannel shirt was soft under her fingertips. "It couldn't have been easy growing up like that."

"No. It wasn't." He seemed frozen in indecision. Olivia knew Cole cared about her, but she also intuitively understood he wasn't willing for those feelings to go any further. "My parents were trapped, and neither would leave, even though it would've been better if they'd called it quits and gotten a divorce. They argued right up to the day they died."

His expression was haunted, and Olivia sensed there was more to the story. But his jaw locked as he held the words back. She wouldn't force him to share more than he was willing. "Is that why you're struggling to write the speech for Eli and Sienna's wedding?"

He nodded. "I'm not good at relationships, Olivia. In fact, I've steered clear of them. Marriage isn't for me." His gaze skittered away from hers. "I'm not sure I even believe that you can be happy for your whole life with someone."

"My grandparents are living proof that not every relationship will end up like your parents."

"They're the exception that proves the rule."

"Are they?" Olivia kept her tone gentle. Challenging Cole's long-held belief needed kindness and understanding. "I don't think so. My grandparents have lots of friends who have been married for decades. Look at your own ranger team. Most of them have caring relationships built on trust and mutual respect."

She knew that for a fact because Olivia had planned two of the weddings herself. Ryker and Hannah wed two years ago. Now Eli and Sienna were poised to walk down the aisle. Both couples had been through difficult times but came out the other side stronger for it. "Marriage can be hard at times, yes, but with the right person—"

He shook his head. "People change, Olivia. I'm not the same as I was ten years ago. I'm sure you aren't either. It's romantic to think a couple can promise to love, honor, and cherish each other, but in actuality, it's a gamble. You don't know what kinds of challenges will come your way. Or how your spouse will react." Cole's mouth flattened as he shifted away from her until the island separated them. A physical and emotional barrier. "I admire your ability to see the best in everyone, but I don't have that skill. I use data and facts. Lots of relationships don't last."

The doorbell rang. Cole's expression shifted as he jumped into Texas Ranger mode. "The team is here. I'll get the door."

He fled the kitchen on long strides. Olivia watched him go, her heart sinking. She didn't believe in changing people. If Cole didn't want a relationship, then she would be wise to listen to him no matter how much it hurt. After her stalker was captured, she and Cole would go their separate ways. The most she could expect was a friendship. And maybe even that was impossible. Her feelings for Cole had grown so much, Olivia wasn't sure she could be around him without hoping for more.

The front door opened. As voices filled the entryway, Olivia braced herself for what lay ahead. Eli and Jackson had spent the afternoon interviewing everyone at Oak Gardens. Had today's attack brought them closer to identifying the stalker?

And if not, what would?

EIGHTEEN

He'd nearly kissed her.

Cole should be thinking about the case, but he couldn't erase the memory of standing in the kitchen with Olivia. The softness of her skin as he brushed the hair from her forehead. Those precious seconds when desire had overtaken his common good sense. He'd stopped himself. But there was no denying his feelings for Olivia were running out of control. Even now, his heart skipped a beat as he accepted the slice of chocolate cake from her.

She wore sweatpants and a T-shirt, her long hair left loose to flow over her shoulders. Her creamy skin was clear of makeup. Their fingers didn't touch, but it seemed every cell in Cole's body wanted to. Olivia, on the other hand, deftly avoided meeting his gaze. She busied herself with cutting another slice of cake and plating it.

Pain and regret smothered the butterflies flitting in his stomach. He set his cake down on the table and crossed the kitchen to fetch the carafe of coffee. It was better this way. Everything Cole said in their conversation was true. He wasn't interested in marriage or a long-term relationship. Too many things could go wrong. His parents' failed marriage taught him that. It wasn't fair to kiss Olivia, to deepen these feelings between them, and then walk away.

Cole poured mugs of coffee and then served his fellow rangers. Dark circles shadowed the skin under Eli's eyes. Jackson's shirt was stained with something that looked like grease, and his hair was mussed, as if he'd been crawling around an attic. The newest member of their team, Felicity Capshaw, waved off the offer of coffee. She'd already poured herself a glass of cold milk to go with her chocolate cake.

Once everyone was settled, Cole shifted the conversation away from small talk and onto the case. "What did you find out during your interviews at Oak Gardens?"

"Someone definitely tampered with the chandelier." Jackson gestured to the grease on his shirt. "I was in the storage unit above the ballroom with the head of maintenance for most of the afternoon. There's a safety mechanism on the motor that runs the pulley system. It prevents the chandelier from hitting the floor even if someone lowers it down. The mechanism was smashed."

Cole figured that was the case, but it was good to have confirmation. "Any idea who might've done it?"

"No. The storage area isn't locked. Anyone could've gone up there. Forensic technicians dusted the door handles for prints but everything was smeared. Not that it would have done us much good if Olivia's stalker is an employee of Oak Gardens, but I was hoping it would narrow the suspect pool down."

"We didn't have any luck with the key or the lockbox on the wall in the ballroom," Eli added. "No fingerprints. And the secretary who works the front desk can't remember the last time she saw the key in the cabinet. Nor can the head of maintenance. We have no idea when the stalker took it. Apparently, that particular key is tucked in the back of the cabinet and is only used when the crew comes to service the chandelier."

Cole's hand tightened on the handle of his coffee mug as frustration bled into his voice. "What about witnesses?"

Felicity frowned. Her dark hair was pulled back into a low ponytail, which she tossed over her shoulder as she cut into her cake. "No one saw anything. I did interview Randy Higgins. He was in the kitchen with half a dozen witnesses when the chandelier fell. He's not our guy."

Olivia sighed. "I don't know whether to be relieved about that or not."

Neither did Cole. "The stalker has to be someone associated with Oak Gardens, right? How else would he have known how to work the chandelier."

"I agree it needs to be someone who's been there and is familiar with the place, but it might not be a current employee." Eli rubbed at his tired eyes. "Oak Gardens has cycled through dozens of waitstaff, maintenance workers, and temporary kitchen help in the last three years. The venue owner, Martha Waterford, provided a list of the current and former employees but it'll take time to go through them all."

Olivia bit her lip. "What about David? He's familiar with Oak Gardens and he's seen how they operate the chandelier. We were there once while a crew was cleaning the crystals."

Jackson shook his head. "David has an alibi."

"Is it his mother?" Cole rolled his eyes.

Every one of the rangers laughed. They all knew that family members often lied for each other to law enforcement.

"Not this time," Jackson said. "David was at the Houston Intercontinental Hotel, attending mandatory new-hire training. Witnesses can place him there during the time of the chandelier incident. He didn't do it."

Olivia shoved aside her uneaten slice of cake. "I don't understand. If David and Randy aren't involved, then where does that leave us?"

"Without a suspect." This time, Cole couldn't keep the frustration from bleeding into his voice. "What about the notes from the stalker? Have forensics found anything that can help us?"

Eli shook his head. "Unfortunately not. The paper can be bought at any major office supply store. The handwriting is consistent, so they were written by the same person, but there were no unknown fingerprints on them. I've reviewed all the evidence Chief Sims collected, as well as everything from the break-in, and the attack on Olivia at the park. We've got nothing solid." He blew out a breath, frustration evident in the crease of his brows.

"We're no closer to identifying the perpetrator than we were a few days ago. Whoever is behind this has covered his tracks very well."

"This definitely isn't his first time. What about the jewelry stolen from Olivia's house?"

"It hasn't shown up at any of the local pawn shops. It's possible he's selling it online." Eli shrugged. "If so, it'll be hard to track."

Cole pushed away from the table. His mind whirled, trying to make sense of what he knew. "Something about this case doesn't add up. I can't figure out why the perpetrator, who'd broken into Olivia's house before, suddenly decided to steal her jewelry. It doesn't jive with the other well-planned attacks."

"Maybe he needs the cash." Jackson sipped his coffee. "Or, like you said the other day, we could be looking at two people."

Felicity made a noise of disagreement. "The stalker is obsessed with Olivia. Someone like that wants to be close to her, wants to touch her things and invade her space. It gives him the high he's looking for. He wouldn't hire someone to do it."

"I agree. All things being equal, a stalker obsessed with his target wants to be close to her." Cole frowned. He'd spent more time thinking about the chandelier incident. His instincts were good, and while Olivia was gorgeous, Cole couldn't accept he was so enraptured that he'd neglected to pay attention to his surroundings. A law enforcement officer never let down his guard. Not even during his personal time. If someone had been watching them from behind the black curtain, Cole was certain he would've felt eyes on him. "But I've been with Olivia for days and haven't spotted anyone watching her. Eli has been out with her many times while planning his wedding and never noticed anyone suspicious."

"What are you saying?"

"When the pieces don't fit, I go back to the beginning and start questioning everything I think I know." Cole drummed his fingers on the table. "We assumed from the notes that we're looking for someone obsessed with Olivia. What if that's wrong? What if the person after her just wants everyone to *believe* she's being stalked?"

The crease in Felicity's brows deepened. "Why would he do that?"

"To cover his tracks. To hide the real motive for hurting Olivia."

Olivia inhaled sharply. Her hand came up to cover her mouth as an expression of horror seeped into her beautiful eyes. "Oh no." She shook her head, as if trying to deny the train of her thoughts. "I... I... no, it couldn't be."

Cole straightened. His pulse picked up speed. "What is it?"

She lowered her hand. Her fingers trembled. "Aaron's brother. His name is Justin Perry. He's currently in state prison, serving fifteen years for a drug charge." Olivia met Cole's gaze. "I'm the reason he's in prison."

Out of the corner of Cole's eye, he spotted Eli take out his cell phone. Probably to do a background check on Justin Perry. Cole focused on Olivia. A flush colored her cheeks and the horrified expression was still etched on her beautiful features. He couldn't bear to see her so upset, and while he didn't like hearing about Justin for the first time now, that fact didn't stop him from reaching for Olivia's hand. "Explain to me why Justin might want to hurt you."

She sucked in a breath and then let it go slowly. "When I was dating Aaron, Justin was in the throes of a gambling addiction. He'd lost his house and was living out of his car. Aaron used to help him out financially but, at some point, had enough. Justin also started using drugs and that's when things got really ugly. Justin threatened Aaron. There were a few fights that nearly came to blows..."

"Over money?"

Olivia nodded. "When Aaron died, Justin found out about the money his brother gave me to start Blessed Events. He snuck up on me after the funeral in the parking lot, high and out of control, and shoved me against the car in front of dozens of people. The cops arrived and arrested him. Turns out, he had a large amount of drugs on him at the time. Enough for a felony charge. He went to prison. He's serving fifteen years."

Jackson whistled. "That's enough to make someone want revenge. If Justin is behind these attacks, he may have hired someone to make it look like Olivia was being stalked. That way no one would ever connect the attacks to him."

Cole agreed. It was the perfect cover-up. He kept his attention locked on Olivia and did his best to keep the recrimination out of his voice. "Why didn't you mention Justin before?"

"Because he's in prison!" The outburst seemed to surprise Olivia because her eyes widened and then her cheeks heated. "I'm sorry. I filed with the Victims Services to be notified when he was released. Since Justin is locked up, it never occurred to me that he could be responsible for all of this."

Her explanation made sense. Olivia didn't work in law enforcement. Cole couldn't be angry with her for not connecting the dots. He hadn't even considered an alternative motive until the second break-in at Olivia's house.

She searched his face. "Do you really think Justin is behind these attacks?"

"It's possible."

"If so, he's hired someone to do his dirty work." Eli tapped his phone screen and then turned it to show Cole. "Justin Perry is currently in state prison serving out his sentence. Does he have any family members or friends who might help him, Olivia?"

"No. His parents are dead and so is Aaron. They didn't have any cousins they were close to." She chewed on her bottom lip. "He did have a girlfriend, but I don't know what happened to her after he was arrested. She didn't come to the trial, so I assume they broke up before then."

"He could've hired a fellow inmate from prison," Cole suggested.

"How would he pay him?" Eli asked.

"Justin inherited some money when his mom died."

Olivia straightened. "She passed away right after Aaron. Justin may have used some of the money for his court case, but his mom's house wasn't sold until after he went to prison. It's my understanding the estate lawyer put the proceeds from the sale into Justin's bank account. Can he access it from prison?"

"Cell phones with internet access are smuggled in and sold on the black market in prison, so yes." Cole met Eli's gaze. "We need a warrant for Justin's bank account and a list of all his visitors. If he hired someone to hurt Olivia, chances are he's communicating with that person somehow. I also want to interview him."

"Why?" Olivia asked.

"Because men like Justin aren't loyal. If we find enough evidence to show he's behind this, and threaten to charge him with attempted murder, he may tell us who his accomplice is." Cole gently squeezed her hand. "My priority is keeping you safe. The best way to do that is by capturing your attacker—"

Cole's cell phone sounded an alarm. He stood and yanked the device from his pocket quickly, accessing the security app for Olivia's house across the street. After the last break-in, he'd installed it on his own phone.

A man in a dark hoodie approached her front door. "Never mind. Maybe we won't have to ask Justin who his accomplice is." He showed the image to Eli and Jackson. "Someone is sneaking up to Olivia's house."

NINETEEN

Olivia paced the length of the living room and then checked her watch. Three minutes. It'd been three minutes since Cole, Eli, and Felicity left to intercept the man nearing her house. She desperately wanted to peek out the front windows to see what was happening, but Jackson had asked her to stay back. He'd stationed himself next to the curtains. From time to time, he parted the blinds to look across the street.

"What's happening?" Olivia's nerves were strung tight. Jackson's attitude only made matters worse. The man was infuriatingly calm. His stance was casual, his long limbs loose. Anyone observing Jackson would think he was watching a friendly football game between neighborhood children, not a potentially deadly interaction with a would-be killer.

"It's too dark and they're in the shadows. I can't tell."

Fresh worry spiked through Olivia. Any more of this stress and her heart would give out.

Jackson released the blinds. They settled back in place as he turned to face her. "Everything's going to be okay."

"How can you know that?" Olivia's hands balled into fists, her nails biting into the tender flesh of her palms. "In the span of twenty-four hours, Cole has been shot at and nearly had a chandelier dropped on his head. He's not a cat with nine lives."

Jackson snorted. "No, but he's not going after the guy alone. He's got Eli and Felicity as backup. All of them are excellent at their jobs." He leveled a knowing gaze in her direction. "You care about Cole, huh?"

This was the second time tonight someone had picked up on her feelings for the handsome Texas Ranger. Granny was forgivable. She knew Olivia well, having raised her since she was fifteen. But Jackson? He'd only met her a few days ago. Under normal circumstances, Olivia would be mortified. Right now, however, all she could think about was Cole's safety.

Her thoughts must've been written on her face, because Jackson nodded as if she'd said the words out loud. "Good. He needs someone like you."

That stopped Olivia in her tracks. "What do you mean?"

"He needs someone who sees that life is more than just the bad things that happen. Someone who operates in joy, but is also fiercely loyal." Jackson turned to peek out the window again. "Cole didn't have the best upbringing, and it messes with his head sometimes. He hasn't had a lot of happiness and he doesn't trust easily."

"Sounds like you can relate."

"No." His voice grew soft. "But I knew a girl just like him once. She succeeded in pushing me away. Sometimes I wish..."

Olivia's heart broke at the regret in his voice. "You wish that you'd fought harder."

He nodded. "We were young. Maybe it still wouldn't have worked out, but at least I would've tried."

She considered the warning coated in Jackson's message. Fear could be an insidious thing. Cole was courageous enough to tackle a killer, but dealing with his own past... that terrified him. She'd seen it in the way he did everything possible to keep up a wall between them. Olivia couldn't change him. If Cole ultimately decided to walk away, then that was his decision. But had she been brave? Had she told him exactly what he was walking away from?

No. She hadn't shared her true feelings with Cole. Olivia wasn't even sure she'd had time to suss out her own emotions with everything going on. What she did know was that she wanted to explore whatever was happening between them.

Maybe when this was all said and done, she'd walk away with a broken heart. But so what? She'd had one before. She'd lost Aaron, her fiancé, the man she was going to spend the rest of her life with. That hadn't destroyed her.

Love required risk. It would take courage to put herself out there and admit she was developing powerful feelings for Cole, but there was no other way. The question was when? This situation was already stressful enough as it was. She didn't want to make things worse by pouring her heart out.

Later. Once the stalker was caught, and she'd had a moment to breathe, then they could have a serious conversation about what they both wanted.

Jackson's posture straightened. "Cole's coming up the sidewalk."

Moments later, he walked in the front door. He wasn't bleeding. No bullet holes or other injuries. Relief washed over Olivia. Before she could think it through, she crossed the room and hugged him. The fabric of his jacket was cold against her bare skin, but when Cole's arms encircled her waist, she felt the warmth of his touch all the way to her core.

She reluctantly pulled back. "What happened? Did you catch the stalker?"

"No." Cole shed his jacket and tossed it on the coat rack next to the door. "The man approaching your house was a neighbor. Danny Myers. He's the fifteen-year-old grandson of Dr. Kenneth Myers."

"I know Dr. Ken. He hosts a block party every year." Olivia frowned. "His grandson lives in West Virginia."

"Yep. Danny is visiting for the weekend. Apparently, Dr. Ken received a delivery sometime this afternoon from a florist. It sat on his porch for hours until Danny came home from running errands and noticed it. Dr. Ken was busy making dinner, so he asked Danny to bring it inside."

Olivia had a sinking feeling she knew where this

story was going. "The flowers were meant for me, weren't they?"

He nodded, his expression grave. "Your name was on the card. They figured the delivery guy had accidentally brought them to the wrong house. Danny was delivering them to you when he was ambushed by three Texas Rangers."

"Poor kid."

Cole's mouth quirked. "He actually took it in stride. Apparently, his maternal grandfather is a retired police officer." He pulled out his cell phone and opened the photos app. A vase of black roses rested on Olivia's front stoop. Tucked inside the blooms was a card addressed to her.

"Black roses. He's not being subtle."

"No, he isn't. Nor is he being careless. Dr. Ken doesn't have security cameras. I believe that's why the stalker dropped the flowers off at his house instead of yours. Eli and Felicity are canvassing the street to see if anyone noticed the delivery man. Or his car. Anything that might provide us with a lead."

Olivia wasn't hopeful. The stalker had proven to be cautious. "He did the same trick with the envelope a few days ago." Her nose wrinkled, thinking of her hand brushing against the dead mouse's fur. Disgusting. "He took it to the barber shop to avoid being seen on the cameras."

Jackson rocked back on his heels. "It's simple and effective. You said Dr. Ken hosts the block parties? He's familiar with the neighbors. Once he saw the name on the card, Dr. Ken knew immediately who to bring it to."

She nodded. "It worked exactly as he intended it to." Olivia's insides crimped with anxiety, but she refused to let it get the best of her. She straightened her shoulders. "What does the note say?"

Cole glanced quickly at Jackson before focusing back on her. "Olivia..."

"No. I want to know. Show it to me, please."

With a sigh, he flipped to a new photograph. Olivia read the message scrawled in block lettering on the note.

Dearest Olivia,

These flowers are a symbol of my feelings for you now—darkened by your betrayal. You chose to run away from our love and hide behind someone unworthy of you. How disappointing. That man can't protect you. He's nothing more than an obstacle, and I've shown you how easily obstacles can be removed. He's still breathing, yes, but that speaks more to my restraint than to his strength.

You must realize by now there's no escape. Every attempt you make to distance yourself from me only makes things worse. You belong to me, Olivia, and no one can change that destiny.

Consider this a warning. My patience wears thin and my generosity has its limits. Do not mistake my love for weakness. Get rid of your assistant or I'll put him in a grave.

Your Devoted Admirer

Her knees trembled. She didn't want the note to affect her, but it did. It sent icy rivers of fear threading through her until she was drowning in worry. Olivia sank down onto the couch cushion and covered her face with her hands. "He's not going to stop."

Cole's warm hand ran down her back in a reassuring gesture as he joined her on the couch. His presence was strong and grounding. A moment later, the front door clicked close. Olivia dropped her hands to find Jackson was gone. He'd slipped out to give them some privacy.

"It's going to be okay, Olivia. This note was sent to scare you."

"Well it's working." She blinked back tears, angry with herself for letting fear get the better of her, but this went beyond her. "By the grace of God, no one was hurt today when the chandelier fell, but what about next time? I can't put innocent people at risk. I'll have to withdraw from the wedding tomorrow. Avery Gonzales will be furious—for good reason—but I can't see any way around it."

"Actually, I've already thought of a game plan. Jackson and Felicity will stay with you while Eli and I go to state prison to interview Justin. Then all four of us will be at the wedding. I doubt the perpetrator will make a move at such a public event, but it's better to be safe than sorry. We'll make sure no one gets hurt."

Olivia wanted to believe him, but doubt held her back. "I'm scared, Cole. What if Justin doesn't tell you who he hired? Or worse, what if he has nothing to do with this?" She gestured to the letter, still on display on Cole's cell phone. "What if the stalker is real, and he intended to make good on his word by killing you?"

"I'm not that easy to kill, if you haven't noticed."

She scowled through her tears. "Now is no time to make jokes."

Cole chuckled and then gently swiped at the water on her cheeks. The smile melted from his face as tenderness took its place. "Nana used to tell me that when things are at their darkest, that's when you need God the most." He cupped her face. "I know you're scared, but we're doing everything we can. Once that's done, then there's only one thing left."

"Prayer." She sighed, touched by his suggestion and the compassionate way he'd handled her fears. Cole had proven he was someone she could lean on over and over again. "Your Nana is very wise."

His lips lifted in a smile that made his eyes sparkle. "You got that right." Cole released her but didn't back away. Instead, her took his hands. "Pray with me, Olivia."

"I'd love to."

TWENTY

The state penitentiary was ice cold. Cole followed Eli into a sterile interview room with cement walls and floor. It stank of urine and sweat. A metal table was bolted to the floor, along with four chairs. The entire space was harsh and unforgiving, devoid of sunlight, illuminated only by the unyielding fluorescent strip of lights embedded in the ceiling. If there was a more depressing place, Cole couldn't imagine it. When the guard shut the door behind them, an irrational sense of claustrophobia swept over him.

"I hate this place," Eli muttered, his mouth set in a grim line. Today he'd worn a dark sports coat with slacks and a button-up shirt. His badge was pinned to the front pocket. The bags under his eyes were deep enough to pack a week's worth of clothes. If Eli kept going at this rate, he was going to look like a mummy at his own wedding next weekend.

Cole wouldn't look much better. Sleep had been

elusive last night. When he wasn't patrolling the Leighton's property, he was lying awake in bed thinking about Olivia. The threats against her were increasing, and Cole felt the incidents were only a hint of what was to come. To make matters worse, his feelings for Olivia were growing beyond what he was capable of hiding. Praying together last night had been intimate. Their hands clasped, heads bowed... he hadn't felt that close to someone in a very long time. And somehow, his deepening friendship with Olivia had also brought him closer to God. He turned to prayer more often, just as his grandmother had urged him to do.

Olivia was quickly becoming a refuge. Someone he could be himself around, share his secrets with, and take care of. He wanted to tell her more about his parents, including his part in the car wreck that'd taken their lives. Cole didn't understand why, but he needed Olivia to understand his resistance to pursuing a relationship had nothing to do with her. It was him.

"You gonna be okay?" Eli's question jolted Cole from his train of thoughts. His friend studied him with consideration. "I don't want you in here if you can't control your temper with Justin."

Cole felt his hackles rise. Eli's comment struck at the core of his fears, that his temper would one day take control of him again. "Since when have I ever lost it?"

"Never, but this case is different. Trust me, I've been there. Sometimes the need to protect the woman you care about overrides common sense."

He opened his mouth to argue but snapped it closed.

There was no sense in denying his feelings for Olivia. Eli knew him too well, and more importantly, there was no judgment or recrimination in his tone. Eli had nearly lost his job and his reputation defending Sienna from a murder charge. Cole blew out a breath. "I've got it under control. You don't have to worry."

The door on the other side of the room opened. Justin, escorted by a prison guard, entered. He'd changed dramatically since the arrest photo. Acne marred his face and muscles in his arms strained the fabric of the standard orange prison garb. His bald head was oily in the harsh fluorescent lighting. Steroids? Cole knew illegal substances—like drugs and cell phones—were smuggled into the prison frequently. A search of Justin's cell hadn't yielded any contraband, but that didn't mean much. He could've hidden it somewhere on the cell block.

Chains jingled as the guard attached Justin's handcuffs to the table. The man didn't seem to mind. He leaned back in the metal chair and smirked. His gaze was flat and cold.

Cole didn't look away. He kept his own face expressionless. With a man like Justin, there was no room for emotion. He'd smell it like a shark smells blood, and then use it to manipulate.

After the guard left, Eli slid into the seat opposite Justin. He introduced himself and Cole. Then he read Justin his rights as required by law.

Justin waved away the warnings. "Yeah, yeah. Whatever." He pulled out an e-cigarette from his shirt pocket and took a drag. "What's this about?"

"Olivia Leighton."

His bored expression didn't change, but there was a flicker of hatred that shifted his flat gaze into one of a cold-blooded individual. Justin took another drag on his e-cigarette. "What about her?"

"Someone has tried to kill her. Several times. We thought you might know something about that."

"How could I? I've been locked up for the last three years."

Justin blew out. The scent of peppermint filled the room. It churned Cole's stomach. He never understood why the state allowed prisoners to buy e-cigarettes from the commissary. "Just because you haven't directly attacked Olivia doesn't mean you aren't responsible. We've done our research, Justin. Fifty grand was moved from your checking account six weeks ago into an off-shore account." Cole locked gazes with the other man. "You hate Olivia. Aaron gave her all his savings, and after his death, you confronted her about it. Witnesses testified that you screamed she'd stolen money you were supposed to inherit after Aaron died."

"And?"

"You attacked her, the police got involved, and they discovered a whole lotta drugs on you, which landed you here. In prison. It's all her fault and I bet sitting in a concrete cage has given you lots of time to think about how to get even. You paid someone to kill Olivia."

Justin's mouth hardened. "Nice little story you got going there, but it ain't true."

"Really?" Eli arched his brows. "Then what was the fifty grand for?"

Justin shrugged. "Some guy I know is buying land in Brazil. It's cheap, but by the time I get out of here, it'll be worth something more. Nothing wrong with investing, is there?"

"How did you move the money?"

"I gave my old lady power of attorney. She took care of it."

His "old lady" was an on-again, off-again girlfriend. "No one has seen or heard from Caroline in weeks. Do you know where we can find her? It would help if she could confirm your story."

"Naw, man." Justin's chains rattled as he lifted his cuffed hands. "In case you haven't noticed, I haven't been out and about. But when you find Caroline, let her know I'm looking for her." He flashed a sharp grin filled with malice.

Cole's stomach sank. He suspected Caroline was dead. Murdered, most likely, but they had no way of proving that. It was possible she'd run off, just as Justin said. He prayed that was the case. "What's the name of the man you gave money to?" He lifted his brows. "Your friend, the investor."

Justin's gaze narrowed. "I'll keep that information to myself."

"That's within your rights." Cole shrugged. "But I wouldn't do that if I were you."

"Why not?"

He moved forward to rest his hands on the back of a

chair. The metal was icy against his heated skin. "Because we're building a case against you, Justin. We know you're involved in these threats against Olivia. Attempted murder charges bring serious time. We're talking twenty-five years to life. Now, if you give us the name of the person you hired, we can work out a deal."

Justin jabbed a stubby finger at his own head. "Are you stupid? I already told ya. I ain't got nothing to do with the attacks against Olivia."

"You threatened her. That's how you ended up in here in the first place."

"Yeah, but that doesn't make me a killer. I was mad about Aaron giving her his money, sure. My brother was a world-class fool when it came to Olivia." Justin smirked. "Aaron never had his life together, but he always lectured me about my choices. The idiot."

His hatred for Aaron and Olivia was barely concealed. It bubbled under the surface. Coupled with the missing fifty grand... yeah, Cole wasn't buying that Justin wasn't involved in the threats against Olivia. Problem was, they didn't have any proof. Justin hadn't had a visitor in months, and the only person he called was his attorney.

Cole was convinced the notes were deliberately planted to make it appear as though Olivia was being stalked. It was a cover-up designed to keep law enforcement looking in the wrong direction. A distraction from the real motive. Revenge.

But how had Justin pulled it off? The only logical conclusion was that he'd hired someone who'd been in prison with him. Thousands of inmates circled through the prison every year. It would take time to identify a potential suspect. They needed a name.

"Olivia hasn't crossed my mind in years," Justin leaned back in his chair and took another drag of his e-cigarette. "I'm busy surviving in this joint. Counting down the days until I get out. After that, I'm starting my life over far away from Serenity and everyone there."

Cole chuckled. "You expect me to believe that you haven't thought about Olivia in *years*? The woman who put you behind bars." He leaned down until he was hovering over Justin. "This isn't going away. I won't stop until I find everyone involved, and once I prove you were a part of it, you're going to spend the rest of your natural life behind bars. Last chance, Justin. Give us the name of the man you hired. End it now."

The younger man glared up at him. His expression was twisted with leashed anger, but a flicker of something flared in his dark eyes. A need for vengeance. Bloodlust. Justin's mouth curled up. "You don't scare me, ranger." He moved into Cole's space, challenging him. "If you had anything solid, we wouldn't be talking."

Cole straightened and then glanced at Eli. "This is a waste of time."

"Sure is." Justin smirked. "These attacks on Olivia, they're a serious concern. One thing I've learned in prison is that once you're a target, it doesn't stop, so you'd better get to work solving the case. Tik tock, ranger." He met Cole's gaze. "Olivia's days are numbered."

TWENTY-ONE

The wedding went off without a hitch.

Olivia breathed a sigh of relief as her clients rushed down the stairs of the Oak Gardens ballroom. Guests waved sparklers and cheered. A truck idled in the circular driveway. It was decked out in streamers and Just Married had been written across the back window. Tail-lights flashed as the couple drove away.

"Another one down." Susan joined Olivia on the stairs. Her secretary wore a gorgeous sheath dress, her curls tucked into a bun. She'd spent the evening helping Olivia coordinate the wedding. It was above and beyond her normal duties, but Susan appreciated the overtime pay. Especially since her husband was still laid up with his bad back. "I'll make sure the bride's parents collect all the gifts before I head home."

"Thank you." Olivia smiled. "Great job, by the way. Sure you don't want to take over as my assistant?"

Susan laughed. "No thanks. I don't want to work

every weekend." Her brows wriggled suggestively. "Besides, you already have an amazing assistant. Where is Cole, anyway? He's been MIA for this evening."

"He wasn't feeling well, and I told him it was okay to skip the wedding." The excuse rolled off Olivia's tongue even as she internally winced. She hated lying, but admitting the truth wasn't possible. Cole and Eli were currently tracking down some leads after their interview with Justin.

Several Texas Rangers—including Jackson and Felicity—provided additional security for the wedding. Olivia hadn't met all the members of Company A, but she'd recognized Grady West and Bennett Knox tucked among the other guests. The latter two lawmen had brought their lovely wives to the event. No one would ever have guessed they were working security.

Susan yawned. "Okay, presents, and then I'm outta here before I fall asleep while driving home. It's way past my bedtime."

Olivia followed her secretary inside. Tables in the ballroom were littered with empty dessert plates and glasses. Silver confetti coated the carpet and dance floor. Guests were gathering their coats and gradually making their way to the parking lot. The DJ was packing up his equipment while waiters cleared the dirty dishes. The broken chandelier had been replaced with one from storage. It didn't have the same sparkle, but it got the job done.

Vincent Santiago, one of Olivia's clients, approached. A friend of the groom, he'd attended the wedding alone.

His fiancée, Rosie, was at home sick with the flu. He'd traded his stained blue jeans for a dark blue suit. His jacket was thrown over one arm and he carried a slice of cake covered with Saran Wrap. "Great wedding. Rosie is going to be sad she missed it."

"I hope she feels better soon. Please send her my love."

"I will." Vincent lifted the plate in his hands, his eyes twinkling with amusement. "It's vanilla. Her favorite."

Olivia laughed. She didn't understand why Cole had been so hard on Vincent. It was clear the man cared a lot about Rosie and did his best to make her happy. Then again, Cole suspected everyone at the moment. Olivia could hardly blame him. Even with Jackson shadowing her every move all evening, she'd been jumpy.

"Are you okay?" Vincent lightly touched Olivia's arm and then immediately dropped his hand. "You zoned out there for a moment."

"Sorry, just thinking." She scanned the ballroom for Jackson but didn't see him. Strange. Maybe he was conducting a patrol of the building. She forced a smile. "Good night, Vincent."

"Night."

After Vincent left, Olivia checked in with the DJ and the event coordinator. Then she headed for the bride's dressing room. It looked like a bomb exploded in there the last time she saw it. The makeup and clothing needed to be gathered together and given to the mother of the bride. Olivia shot off a text letting Jackson know where she would be as she exited the ballroom. Quiet descended the farther into the building she went. The bride's dressing room was around another bend.

Olivia's heels sank into the plush carpet. Then she drew up short. Her former assistant, David, was standing near an exit leading to the side parking lot, speaking on his cell phone. His dark suit was pressed and his hair was combed back neatly. A diamond earring winked from his earlobe. In these clothes, he looked like a different person. More like the man she knew.

He spotted her and hung up. "Hey, Olivia. Outstanding wedding. From start to finish, it was sheer perfection." His expression turned wistful. "I'm gonna miss working on these weddings together. We made a great team."

His compliment was so genuine, Olivia felt a pang of regret. How could she ever have believed David was her stalker? His alibi on the night of the second break-in at her house had officially cleared him from the suspect list. And she was relieved. "I'm going to miss it, too, but you're on to better things, and I couldn't be happier for you."

"Thanks. The event coordinator position is going to keep me busy, but I'm excited about the challenge. Don't know how many more of these weddings I'll be available to attend though. Several of Blessed Event's clients have invited me, but my new schedule requires a lot of evenings and weekends."

"Susan and I were just discussing that." Olivia sighed. When this was all said and done, she'd have to find a new assistant. A real one this time. It was exhausting to think about. "Let me know if anyone from the hotel is looking for a change. A small-town job with decent pay and a nice boss."

David laughed. "I will." He paused and then tilted his head. "Cole not working out?"

"I don't know. We'll see how long he sticks around."

David made a sound of agreement. "I warned him you were a perfectionist."

Olivia chuckled. She couldn't deny it. "It was good to see you, David." She gestured to the bride's room. "I better get a move on, otherwise I'll be here all night."

"Sure, sure." David walked off but then stopped and turned. His expression was intense. "You look great tonight, Olivia. Real pretty."

Her pulse fluttered as fear jolted through her veins. She felt trapped in David's stare, and suddenly, Olivia became all too aware of how isolated they were in the hallway. Would anyone hear her if she screamed? She wasn't sure. Primal instinct caused her to take a step back as David re-approached. Her back bumped against the wall.

He had her cornered.

David seemed oblivious to her terror. He stopped a short distance away, just shy of invading her personal space. "Listen, I know this sounds forward, but would you consider grabbing a bite to eat with me? Angie and I have been having more trouble. In fact, she broke up with me. It's official. We're done. You're nice and I enjoy talking to you. With everything going on, I could really use a friend."

He has an alibi. He has an alibi.

The words played like a mantra in her head as she attempted to wrangle her emotions under control. There was no logical reason to be afraid of David, but there was something about the intense way he was looking at her. Like she was prey. It was unnerving and made her question everything she knew.

Could she outwardly reject him? If David was her stalker, saying no could send him into a rage. Olivia could scream for help, and eventually someone would come, but that wouldn't stop a bullet. Or a knife. David's hand was in his pocket. Did he have a weapon? Olivia's mind jumped from thought to thought, fear causing her heart to jackhammer against her chest.

God, help me find the right words.

Olivia licked her lips. "Sorry, David, I've got so much to do tonight. In fact, I need to check on Susan. She's supposed to be taking care of the gifts, and I don't want her to forget any." She slid along the wall, inching away from him. Her heart thundered. It was loud. Olivia was terrified he'd hear it. "Let's take a rain check on dinner."

She had no intention of eating with him. Ever. But he didn't need to know that.

David's gaze narrowed. "I thought you were going to the bride's dressing room."

"I will. After I check on Susan."

Olivia slid to the side, skirting around David. She half expected his hand to clamp down on her arm, but it didn't. Once a path was clear, Olivia bolted.

David called out.

She ignored him. The need to put distance between

them was instinctive and overwhelming. Safety, and people, were a short distance away in the ballroom. Olivia rounded the corner at full speed. Her body collided with something solid, knocking her back. Her hair, left loose, flew into her face, blocking her vision. Hands grabbed her arms. David? Had he gone the back way in order to intercept her?

Olivia screamed.

TWENTY-TWO

"Olivia!"

Her hair was in her face, and she was on autopilot, struggling against his hold. Cole dodged Olivia's knee as it came up. He released her, once again calling her name. She didn't seem to hear him. Her blood-curdling scream brought Texas Ranger Grady West racing around the corner just as a kick landed on Cole's shin. The pointy part of her high heel sent pain shooting up his leg.

He took another step away from her. The hallway behind her was empty. What on earth had scared her so badly? "Olivia, stop. It's Cole."

She froze. Strands of hair fluttered with each one of her heaving breaths. She tossed the caramel mane out of her face and finally registered his presence. Relief, so potent it made Cole's heart ache, melted the fear from her face. He reached for her, lightly grasping her biceps. "What happened?"

"David." She pointed with a shaking finger down the hallway.

Grady didn't need any additional information. The ranger took off in pursuit, his boots pounding against the carpet.

Cole opened a door next to them. It was a small conference room. He steered a trembling Olivia inside. Her complexion was ghostly pale, and he feared she might faint. Adrenaline caused a fight-or-flight response, but after the incident was over, it left a person weak-kneed and exhausted. To make matters worse, Olivia hadn't been sleeping well. The sheer amount of stress she'd been under was enough to make anyone crumble.

He pulled out a chair. "Here. Sit."

She ignored his order, instead wrapping her arms around his waist. Cole immediately responded by pulling her close. Olivia fit against him perfectly, as if she'd been made for him. He brushed a kiss across her temple. The scent of her shampoo—something light and floral—was now familiar after all the time they'd spent together recently. Olivia's breathing steadied. Cole gently ran a hand up and down her spine in a soothing motion. Questions needed to be asked, but they could wait.

Right now, he was going to comfort her. And thank God that she was okay.

Half an hour later, Cole stood in the hallway outside the conference room with Grady. His friend and colleague was grim-faced. His suit was stained with dirt and the fabric over one knee was ripped. He'd tackled David in the parking lot before escorting him back inside. Ranger Bennett Knox was questioning the man in an empty office a few doors down.

"Felicity and Jackson are on their way to the hospital." Grady scraped a hand through his dark hair before replacing his cowboy hat. "Tara found Felicity violently throwing up inside the bathroom just as the newly married couple was leaving for their honeymoon."

Dr. Tara West was Grady's wife. Currently, she was inside the conference room with Olivia. The door wasn't shut all the way, leaving a crack big enough to observe them. Tara held Olivia's hand and was quietly talking. Or maybe they were praying. Tara's faith ran deep. She'd started a prayer chain for members of Company A, and as each ranger married and their families grew with children, she extended it to them as well.

"Tara alerted me," Grady continued. "Then I found Jackson passed out in the men's room. He'd started a text, but hadn't been able to send it. Tara suspects they were both drugged based on the symptoms. Her best guess is that something was dusted onto their slices of wedding cake, probably powdered fentanyl since it's tasteless and odorless. Jackson ate his entire slice of cake, which is why his symptoms were worse. Felicity only had a few bites of hers."

Anger shot through Cole and his muscles went rigid. "Do we know who's responsible?"

"No. I reviewed the security footage, but the waiter

who handed them the cake slices kept his head down the whole time. It doesn't look like someone who works here because he doesn't appear in the kitchen until halfway through the reception. He delivered a few meals, and then the cake slices to Jackson and Felicity. He left after that."

Grady tapped on his phone and brought up an image on the screen. It was a still taken from the video footage. A man, dressed in a waiter's uniform, kept his head down as if he was studying his shoes. Cole estimated he was around six foot. Mud-colored, straight hair.

He squinted. "Is he wearing a wig?"

"Yes. Felicity was able to give us a brief description. She said he had a mustache and beard, looked fit, and moved with confidence. He also wore glasses. Something about him didn't sit right with her the first time she spotted him, so she kept an eye on him during the reception. He remained professional and didn't seem out of place. Some of the other servers even chatted with him. We're conducting interviews now to see what was discussed, but so far, it was mundane stuff." Grady flipped to another photograph taken from the video footage. "But look at this."

The culprit stood at the edge of the ballroom with a tray. He was within five steps of Olivia's makeshift command station behind the DJ booth. Although his face was turned down to avoid the cameras overhead, his attention was locked on Olivia, who was busy talking with Susan about something.

Cole's hands balled into fists. He'd heard the saying

"seeing red" but had only experienced it once in his life. The night his parents died. Now, his temper spiked to a level he hadn't known was possible. Somewhere in the recesses of his mind, an alarm bell went off. He gritted his teeth and sucked in a breath. "Who is he?"

"We don't know. Chief Sims found the wig, mustache, and glasses in the dumpster outside. We've sent it to the lab for processing. Hopefully, we'll get some DNA from it." Grady zoomed in on the image. "Is it possible this man is David?"

He studied the culprit, willing his temper back under control. "They have the same size and build, but it's hard to say definitively since his face is turned down."

At that moment, Eli came around the corner. Along-side him was Texas Ranger Bennett Knox, another member of Company A. They joined Cole and Grady outside the conference room. Grady filled them in on what they knew so far.

Bennett gestured to the man in the photo. "I doubt that's David. Emilia and I spent the last half hour inter-viewing him." Emilia Sanchez was Bennett's wife. She was an expert profiler with the state police. "David says that Olivia freaked out after he asked her to have dinner. He was shocked by her behavior. When we shared she was being stalked, he seemed genuinely surprised. I don't think he intended to upset her."

"That makes some sense, since David has an alibi for one of the break-ins at Olivia's house," Eli added. "He was doing new-hire training at the Intercontinental

Hotel. We have witnesses that confirm it and security footage that backs the alibi up."

Cole's jaw tightened. The analytical side of him knew his colleagues were right. It was possible David had nothing to do with the attacks against Olivia, but he couldn't shake the feeling that things weren't that simple. "I don't want to mark him off the suspect list because of his alibi. Not yet. The last break-in at Olivia's house—the one David has an alibi for—included theft. The perpetrator stole jewelry. He'd never done that before, even though he'd been in her house multiple times. I still think we could be dealing with two different people."

Bennett rocked back on his heels. "I'll ask Emilia to do a complete workup on the case. She can give us a profile of the stalker and confirm or refute Cole's suspicions about the second person."

Cole shot his colleague a grateful look. "I appreciate it."

"What about the chef?" Grady asked. "Randy Higgins is a suspect, right? He could've easily poisoned the cake slices."

"Except he was in the kitchen with dozens of employees when this waiter"—Eli pointed to Grady's cell phone. The image of the man in glasses was still on display—"delivered the cake slices to Jackson and Felicity."

"Yeah, but if we're dealing with two different perpetrators, as Cole suggests, then Mr. Glasses could be working with the chef. Randy drugs the cake slices and Mr. Glasses delivers them."

He had a good point. Cole considered the options. "We need to be careful before eliminating anyone off the suspect list. Let's review all the footage from today. Track Mr. Glasses' movements and interview everyone he interacted with. The priority is IDing him. Fifty grand was withdrawn from Justin's bank account one week before someone started stalking Olivia. It went to an off-shore account, so we can't trace it." Cole growled in frustration. "The way I see it, we have two possibilities. One, Mr. Glasses was hired by Justin to stalk and eventually kill Olivia. This setup is designed to hide Justin's involvement and make it look like Olivia's death was the result of a stalker, when it was actually about revenge."

Eli nodded, his mouth set in a grim line. "Justin wants revenge, that much is certain. He hates Olivia and blames her for his prison sentence."

"Exactly. The second possibility is that Olivia is truly being stalked—either by David or Randy—and the fifty grand withdrawn from Justin's account is a happenstance."

Bennett snorted. "I don't believe in coincidences."

"Neither do I, but Justin is a criminal. It's possible the money has nothing to do with Olivia and he's involved in some other shady dealing." Cole wouldn't dismiss any plausible theory. Doing so could cause him to overlook an important clue that would blow the entire case wide open. He pointed to the man on Grady's cell phone screen. "We need to identify Mr. Glasses. We know he's involved. Once we learn his identity, hopefully we can figure out who he's connected to."

Cole surmised Mr. Glasses had drugged Jackson and Felicity in order to get Olivia alone. Anything could've happened tonight. Cole didn't know what the perpetrator planned, but he had a feeling his arrival at Oak Gardens had stopped it. "We should review the security footage for anyone who attended the wedding but disappeared when Mr. Glasses showed up, and then reappears after he left. It's possible he's been here the whole time."

"Good idea." Grady rocked back on his heels. "I'll do that."

As much as Cole hated to pull Olivia away from a job she loved, and one she was exceedingly good at, things had gone too far. "And until we have a better handle on this case, Olivia needs to step back from her business. There's too much risk to innocent people. And to her."

Eli nodded. "I agree. Her next wedding is mine and Sienna's. Hopefully, we'll solve this case before next weekend, but if we don't, we'll just make do."

"We can do better than that." Tara stepped out of the conference room. The sequins on her navy blue dress sparkled in the light. "I spoke with Olivia and she's given me all the necessary details to make Sienna and Eli's wedding a success. Everyone will pitch in to help. Megan, Avery, Claire, Emilia, and Hannah have already replied to my SOS message. We'll see to the final details and the wedding will be a resounding success."

The tension eased from Eli's shoulders, and he gave Tara a brotherly one-armed hug. "Thank you. It means a lot to me. And I know it'll help calm Sienna's nerves. Olivia's been instrumental in keeping Sienna sane during the planning process. There's so much to do this week, and since I'm in charge of this case, I won't be much help."

"We're all happy to chip in. Leave everything to me." Tara tilted her head as she moved closer to her husband. She took the phone from Grady's hand. "Has anyone shown this picture to Olivia? When I was stalked, it was by someone I knew. Chances are this guy has been up close to her at some point... interacted with her..." Her brow crinkled as she gazed up at her husband. "Isn't that what fuels the stalker?"

"Normally, yes, but this case isn't stereotypical."

"Still, Tara has a point." Cole slid his own phone out of his pocket as he glanced in the conference room. Olivia was staring out the window at the fountain. "Send me the picture. I'll run it by Olivia."

The sooner they identified Mr. Glasses, the better. Justin's warning haunted Cole.

Tik tock, ranger.

Olivia's days are numbered.

TWENTY-THREE

The fountain in the lake sprayed water high into the air. The falling droplets shimmered in the golden bask of lighting that came from a bulb underneath the surface. An hour ago, Olivia had felt in control. Any problem that arose—from the DJ's song selection to a rip in the bride's dress—was manageable. Now she felt like those water droplets tumbling through the air. Completely upended.

She closed her eyes. Her heart ached as guilt plagued her. Although Olivia knew she wasn't responsible for what happened to Jackson and Felicity, she still felt awful. They'd been injured while protecting her.

Lord, please watch over Jackson and Felicity. Keep them safe as they recover. Guide the doctors and the nurses at the hospital so they can provide the best care. Amen.

"Olivia?"

She opened her eyes and turned to find Cole standing a few paces away. Olivia offered him a weak smile. "I was praying for Jackson and Felicity. Is there any news about their condition?"

"Not yet. Tara is going to the hospital. She'll text us with an update." He drew closer, his expression etched with understanding. "If it helps, Tara believes they'll make a full recovery. They were both conscious and responding well to treatment after the paramedics arrived."

"She told me as much. Still, extra prayers can't hurt, right?"

"No, prayers are always welcome." Cole joined her at the window. He held his cell phone in one hand. "I have something I need to show you." He tapped on the screen, bringing up a photograph. "Have you ever seen this man before tonight?"

Olivia carefully studied the image. The man's face wasn't visible, but she could tell he was wearing glasses. Nothing about him seemed familiar. She shook her head. "I don't think so. Why?"

"We believe he's the one who drugged Jackson and Felicity." Cole frowned. "Take another look. I know it's hard because his facial features aren't clear. Keep in mind that his hair color might've been different when you saw him. We found a wig, glasses, and a mustache in a nearby dumpster."

"He used a disguise?" Shock vibrated through Olivia, although it probably shouldn't have. Her stalker had proven to be industrious and intelligent. A memory wriggled at the edge of her mind. She frowned, willing it forward, but it slipped away. Olivia sighed with frustration. "I'm sorry. Without being able to see more of his face, it's impossible to say whether I've seen him before or not."

"It's okay."

She frowned. "I don't understand. If this guy drugged Jackson and Felicity, then how does David fit into all of this?"

"We're still looking into that." Cole clicked his phone off. He pulled out a chair. "Sit down. I'll fill you in on everything we know."

For the next five minutes, Olivia listened without interrupting. She waffled between confusion, horror, and anger. Especially when Cole told her about his visit with Justin. She'd never liked Aaron's brother and had long suspected he was involved in more than just drugs.

"There's something I need to tell you." Olivia licked her lips. "After Aaron died, I asked Chief Sims to investigate the matter. Aaron was violently allergic to bees and was careful to steer clear of them. We'd been in the shed a few days before his death. There was no beehive."

Cole's eyes widened. "Are you saying that Justin killed his brother?"

"I had a suspicion. Justin had asked Aaron for money but was refused. He got angry about it. Then a few days later, he showed up at Aaron's house and apologized. They hung out together for a while. Two days later, Aaron was dead. He had an EpiPen in his house, near the back door. Another in the living room. Aaron was careful because he knew his allergy was serious. The EpiPen next to the back door had been moved to the medicine cabinet." She balled her hands into fists, mentally berating herself for not pushing Chief Sims to investigate her fiancé's death more. "Bees can be ordered from beekeepers online. I know. I researched it after Aaron died and took the information to Chief Sims."

Cole's mouth twisted. "And he didn't look into the matter?"

"No. I should've pushed harder, fought more, but he assured me Aaron's death was a tragic accident. I was grief stricken and had been threatened by Justin after the funeral..." Olivia had barely had the strength to get out of bed and face the day. She'd been drowning in memories. It was shameful to admit just how lost she'd been. How weak. "Losing Aaron was painful. I'd loved him deeply. His death also dragged up a lot of buried anguish about my parents. I was a mess, and I can't blame Chief Sims for dismissing my claims as the ramblings of a distressed woman."

"I can." Cole gently placed a hand over hers. "You might've been grieving, but I doubt anyone would ever accuse you of illogical ramblings. And it's Chief Sims's job to thoroughly investigate. He should've taken your observations more seriously, especially after Justin's attack on you after the funeral, when he discovered he wasn't inheriting Aaron's money."

She stared at their joined hands before lifting her gaze to his. His words touched something inside her that she hadn't realized was hurting. "You give me too much credit. I'm a lot weaker than you realize."

"Weak?" His tone was incredulous. "You're one of

the strongest people I know." Cole's mouth quirked. "And if you want proof, take a look at my shin. I've got a bruise the size of an apple on it. Those heels don't just make your legs look gorgeous, they're excellent weapons."

Olivia laughed in spite of the seriousness of their conversation. "I'm sorry. Did I really bruise you?"

He waved away her concern. "I'm fine." Cole squeezed her hand, and the warmth emanating from his dark brown eyes nearly undid her. "You have been through one tragedy after another, but you're still standing tall. You've built a successful business from the ground up. I've seen you wrangle a difficult mother-in-law with a smile, help a couple pick a wedding cake, and take care of your grandparents, all while being stalked by an unknown man. You're incredibly brave, Olivia. Don't ever let anyone tell you otherwise."

Her breath hitched. Olivia realized her heart was on the cusp of falling for the handsome Texas Ranger sitting at her side, but like everything else happening at the moment, she felt powerless to stop it. He was her anchor in the storm. Her protector. Cole's caring nature, his faith, and the unwavering commitment to his job were admirable qualities. Over and over again, he'd proven to be someone she could rely on. Olivia didn't have the strength or the energy to keep fighting these feelings for him.

She leaned forward and brushed her mouth against his. Cole tensed for half a heartbeat, and then he rose from his chair, pulling her into a standing position. His lips claimed hers.

Molten lava slid through her veins and her knees weakened. Oh mercy, the man could kiss. Olivia lifted her hands to his broad shoulders as he deepened the kiss, gently leading her to a world only they knew. She lost herself in the sensations pouring through her. The feel of his lips against hers, the scent of his aftershave, the reverence of his touch.

When the kiss was over, Cole pulled away breathless. He looked as stunned as Olivia felt. She wasn't a shy schoolgirl encountering her first kiss, but a mature woman. Still, she'd never experienced anything like this before. Their friendship and trust had deepened quickly amid the threats. It'd fueled an attraction stronger than she'd imagined possible.

"Olivia…" Cole brushed a thumb across her bottom lip. Then he released her. "I'm sorry. I shouldn't have done that."

No. She wasn't going to let him run away from this conversation. Things had gone too far, and Olivia hadn't misconstrued the passion they shared. It wasn't one-sided. He cared about her. She knew that with every breath in her body.

Olivia put a hand on his chest. "We just shared something very special, so if you're saying it shouldn't have happened, I need more of an explanation."

He pulled away and went to the window. The line of his back was rigid. "I told you. I don't believe in marriage. My house was like a war zone when I was a kid. I refuse to make the same mistake they did." Cole's voice softened. "I'm just like them. I have that temper inside of me."

If that was true, she'd never seen a glimpse of it. Olivia wanted to comfort him but kept her distance, sensing Cole couldn't accept her touch. Not yet. "What do you mean by that?"

"The night of their car crash... my parents were arguing. It started off about money but quickly dissolved into my dad's infidelity and my mom's disloyalty. I was in the back seat and couldn't take it anymore. I yelled at them to stop. Screamed actually. I don't know... something came over me and I couldn't control the words coming out of my mouth. My parents both started hollering at me to shut up. I wouldn't though. And then my dad turned around to smack me across the face."

Inside, Olivia was seething that Cole, as a little boy, had grown up in such an environment. But he didn't need her outrage. He needed her compassion and understanding.

Cole turned to face her. "That's when the accident happened. My dad crossed the yellow line into oncoming traffic. My parents died. I didn't."

His tone was hollow, but underneath, she heard the tears he held back. Her heart broke. "You aren't responsible for what happened. You know that, don't you?"

"I screamed at them. I lost my temper." He crossed his arms over his chest. "Their anger problems... they live inside me too. I'm capable of hurting the people I love."

"No, Cole." Now Olivia did draw closer, unable to keep the distance between them. She came to a stop in front of him. "You were a terrified child who reacted to his parents' heated argument. That's all. You aren't to blame for their deaths, and I don't believe for a moment that you have an anger management problem. I've seen you in deadly confrontations with a criminal and you've never acted blindly."

A muscle in his jaw twitched. He didn't say anything.

She touched his arm. The muscles were stiff under her palm. "I know exactly who I kissed. You're a good man, Cole. Your parents had a bad marriage and I can understand how that affected you, but things can be different. They already are. Look at us."

He was quiet for a long moment and then shook his head. "You don't understand. My parents loved each other once too." Cole tenderly cupped her cheek. "I don't want to hurt you, Olivia."

This man... he wasn't trying to be difficult or stubborn. He was protective, right down to his core, and Olivia's heart expanded. The fact that Cole was worried about hurting her was a testament to how much he cared. "You would never purposefully hurt me. You aren't like your parents."

"I wish I could believe that." He sighed. "It's late and I'm tired. So are you. Let's go."

She hesitated and then nodded. They'd been through a lot tonight, and while she hated leaving things so conflicted, continuing this conversation when they were both emotionally wrung out would make things worse instead of better.

The night air was frigid as Olivia walked beside Cole

to his truck. Serenity Police Department cruisers sat next to official state patrol vehicles in the parking lot. A physical reminder of the stalker that'd come breathtakingly close to her tonight. A shudder rippled down Olivia's spine. How much longer could this go on?

Cole's cell phone beeped with an incoming text as he hopped into the driver's seat. He scanned it. "Jackson and Felicity are both stable. The doctor wants to keep them overnight for observation, but barring any unforeseen complication, they should be discharged tomorrow."

"Thank God." She reached into her purse and pulled out a pair of tennis shoes, quickly trading them for her high heels. Her aching feet instantly felt better.

Olivia settled against the seat as Cole fired up the engine. The heaters blasted warm air, erasing the chill, and country music softly played from the radio. Exhaustion seeped into Olivia's muscles. The silence between her and Cole wasn't tense. More reflective. She sensed he was mulling over their conversation. Or maybe the case. Darkness surrounded the vehicle as they drove down the country roads toward home. In the distance, lightning flared. A storm was coming. She closed her eyes and drifted.

"Olivia!" Cole's tense tone jolted her out of a light sleep. He gently pushed her head toward her knees. "Get down!"

The back window of the truck exploded.

TWENTY-FOUR

Fire blazed through Cole's right arm. Warm liquid, running fast, coated his shoulder.

He'd been shot.

The pain was nothing compared to the knowledge that their attacker was closing in fast once again. Air rushed into the truck through the shattered back window. Cole's attention was locked on his rearview mirror. Headlights from a dark-colored SUV raced toward them. "Stay down, Olivia!"

She was bent over at the waist with a cell phone in her hand. A second later, he heard the brilliant woman communicating with Eli. Cole jammed on the accelerator, but the vehicles were well-matched. A roar came behind them seconds before metal pinged. He was shooting at them again.

Cole swerved. Agony shot through his arm. The fingers on his right hand were numb, forcing him to use only his left to drive. There was no way to outrun the attacker, and they were miles from civilization. This stretch of two-lane country road didn't even have street-lights. There was nothing but trees, cow fields, and a small recreational fishing lake. His speed climbed danger-ously high.

Another roar erupted. Cole glanced in the rearview mirror in time to see the headlights zooming close. His heart rate spiked as he instinctively understood the other driver's intentions. He was going to hit them. "Hold on, Olivia."

Metal crunched as the vehicles collided, and his head hit the back of the seat. The tires slid against the wet asphalt and then caught. A horn blared. Olivia screamed as headlights from an oncoming vehicle flooded their truck. Cole swiftly maneuvered back into the correct lane, his heart racing. A moving van whizzed past them.

Close. Too close. The SUV hadn't made full impact with their vehicle, but a high-speed chase threatened too many lives. Theirs. Innocent civilians. Cole racked his brain for an escape route, but couldn't figure out one that would work. He glanced in the rearview mirror. The SUV lingered behind them. As if the driver was consid-ering his next move.

The rain picked up, battering against the windshield. Cole knew he should slow down, but couldn't. His arm was now completely numb. Blood gushed from the wound, coating his skin and his hand. The frigid air rushing in through the back window blew Olivia's hair around her face. Her eyes were wide and her fingers clutched the cross bracelet at her wrist. Terrified. She was terrified. Cole wanted to comfort her, but another roar from the truck behind them jerked his attention back to the danger at hand.

He was going to hit them again. Cole slammed on the accelerator, and the SUV kissed their bumper. Then the driver zoomed into the next lane. His engine revved. Glass shattered as a bullet busted through the extended cab's side window. The stalker was shooting at him. Cole grimaced and tightened his hold on the steering wheel. A thump, thump came from the tire. Shoot. They had a flat.

A bend in the road preceded a small bridge over a creek. There was only one option. He eased off the gas and let the SUV edge closer. Timing was everything.

Wait for it... wait.... He glanced at Olivia. "Brace yourself. Bend over and cover your head with your hands."

She gave a sharp nod and then did as instructed. Trust emanated from that simple action. It added fuel to Cole's already raging protective instincts. He wouldn't let anyone harm her. He'd die first. *God, please let this work.*

Cole glanced at the side-view mirror. Another bullet pinged off the metal. His fingers tightened on the steering wheel. Almost there... a bit more... He eased off the gas again and the SUV's bumper was nearly at the driver's side door.

Without warning, Cole hit the brakes. Smoke rose from the tires as the truck went from 90 miles an hour to almost nothing. They hydroplaned on the wet road while the SUV zoomed ahead. The driver tried to take the turn at the bridge but failed. The SUV veered toward the ditch and then hit a tree.

Any relief was short-lived. The steering wheel shuddered under Cole's hand. A tire exploded under the force of his emergency brake maneuver and they fishtailed uncontrollably. The truck went into a spin. Cole desperately pumped the brakes to regain control, but it was no use. Trees whirled and then they were tumbling off the road.

Metal screeched and glass shattered as the truck tumbled off a small embankment. Cole's head smashed against the side panel. Pain erupted and spots danced across his vision. The seat belt gripped him like a vise. He couldn't breathe. Couldn't move. Objects from the cup holders and the side pockets flew around him. Agony screamed through his body as his gunshot wound was jostled violently.

The truck came to a shuddering stop. Cole blinked, wondering if he'd passed out momentarily. The dots in his vision wouldn't fade. He tried to suck in a breath, but only managed a wheeze. "Olivia." Panic rose in his chest when she didn't answer. He twisted his head to look at her, his neck protesting even that slight movement. Her seat was empty. "Olivia!"

"I'm here." She appeared at his broken window. Cole couldn't make out her features in the dark, but a second later, his door swung open. By some miracle, it still worked. Then her hands were touching him. "You passed out. I found the first aid kit under my seat. You've been shot."

"I know." He blinked to clear his vision, even as he reached for her. "Are you hurt?"

"I'm fine, just bruises."

Her face swam in front of him. Cole could barely make out the faint scratches on her cheek. Her hair was damp from the rain. She undid the top buttons on his shirt and then the sound of a package being ripped open preceded white-hot pain as she pressed a bandage to his gunshot wound. He couldn't feel anything past his shoulder. His fingers were completely numb. Darkness threatened to take him back under, but Cole fought against it. "We can't stay here. We're sitting ducks."

She tensed. "You think he'll come after us? But he was in an accident. I saw it."

So did Cole, but the SUV had a strong grill on the front of it. The accident probably amounted to little more than a fender bender. Every second counted. The man could be headed their way right now, armed and ready to take Olivia by any means necessary. "Do you know where your cell phone is? Or mine?"

"My cell was crushed in the accident and doesn't work. I haven't seen yours."

It'd been in the cup holder before the accident and could be anywhere in the vehicle. They didn't have time to hunt for it. Cole fumbled with his seat belt, finally finding the release. "We have to move." Backup was on the way, since Olivia had called Eli before the accident, but it would take them time to get there.

"Wait, you've lost a lot of blood."

She opened another bandage and then quickly

looped it over and around his shoulder to help slow the bleeding. The pain from his wounds, and the adrenaline running through his veins, heightened all his senses. Her touch was efficient but gentle, and when she was done, Olivia brushed her mouth against his. A light kiss, softer than the rain pattering against the leaves of the tree, but the emotion behind it was enough to send Cole's heart racing all over again.

"Susan and her husband have a vacation rental nearby." Olivia lowered herself to the ground. "This time of year, no one occupies it. We can hide there until help arrives."

Cole gritted his teeth and climbed out of the wrecked truck. He swayed, his vision once again swimming. Bile rose in the back of his throat. "If I pass out, keep moving."

"I won't do that, so you'd better not pass out." Olivia looped his good arm around her shoulders. "Lean on me."

Together, they made their way to the tree line. Cole paused, glancing over his shoulder. The rain and his blurred vision prevented him from seeing the road, but Olivia's sharp inhale told him everything. The stalker was coming. Hunting them.

Hunting her.

"Keep moving," Cole ordered. He focused on putting one foot in front of the other. Leaves crunched under his boots. The rain soaked his hair and dropped water down the back of his collar. Icy wind rustled the tree leaves. He hoped the weather shrouded their movements. At some point, he stopped. Listened. It didn't sound like anyone was following them, but he couldn't be sure.

Cole leaned against a tree and used his left hand to unhook the button on his holster. He couldn't slide the weapon out due to the awkward angle. Olivia, obviously understanding his intention, removed the gun and handed it to him. Wordlessly, he took it. He'd never shot using his left hand, probably couldn't hit the broad side of a barn, but having hold of the weapon instantly made him feel more secure.

A twig snapped.

Cole stiffened. His gaze scanned the woods. An animal? Or the stalker?

Silence stretched out. Then a deer stepped out from the shelter of a nearby bush. Cole let go of the breath he was holding. "Let's keep going."

"It's not far."

Cole tried to walk on his own, but the world still swam in front of his eyes. He had a concussion. Olivia once again resumed her place as his crutch. Her slender form was strong, her steps sure. Frustration at his lack of capabilities dug into him like claws, but the emotion was useless given the circumstances. Olivia wouldn't leave without him. She was stubborn enough—and brave enough—to risk her life to save his. It was a shame she couldn't shoot. Willie had tried to teach her many times, but Olivia said she'd never felt comfortable with a gun.

A small house appeared ahead with a dirt driveway leading up to the main road. The lake was on their left, a dark black blob against the backdrop of pine trees. Olivia and Cole circled the building, stopping at the front stoop.

He was panting. Despite the cold nighttime air, and the drizzle, sweat gathered at the base of his spine.

"Wait a second." Olivia unhooked Cole's arm from around her shoulders and began digging in the flowerbed. She flipped over a rock and then rose, a triumphant look on her face. "Keys."

He kept watch while she opened the front door. The house was warmer than the outdoors and smelled musty. Cole locked the door with a trembling hand and gave his eyes a moment to adjust to the dark interior. A couch hulked in the corner opposite a modestly sized television. A kitchen was on their left. A hallway, probably leading to the bedrooms, was on their right.

"Come on." Olivia grabbed his arm. Her hand was chilled. "We have to get dry, and I need to take a closer look at that wound. Then I'll hunt around for a way to call Eli. Susan mentioned her husband keeps a satellite phone here for emergencies."

Cole's teeth chattered as he lowered himself to the bathroom floor. Olivia dried off his hair and then helped him remove his jacket. She winced at the blood coating his shirt. It had dripped all the way down the front and along the sleeve, but her makeshift bandage at the car had slowed some of the blood loss. He grabbed her hand before she could examine him further.

"I'm fine. Dry yourself off and get the satellite phone." Olivia looked like she wanted to argue, but he kissed her palm. "Please. Contacting Eli is the most important thing. The sooner we have backup here, the better."

Cole didn't mention that his head was spinning. He couldn't protect her like this if the stalker found them. He needed backup. His grip on the gun was weak. With his blurry vision and injured shoulder, he was practically useless.

Olivia's expression softened. She covered him in dry towels. "I'll be right back."

She slipped from the bathroom. Cole's trembling increased. He'd held it together in front of Olivia, but the blood loss coupled with the concussion had sapped most of his strength. Leaning his head against the bathtub, Cole closed his eyes. He needed to rest. Just for a moment.

Darkness claimed him.

TWENTY-FIVE

She couldn't find the satellite phone.

Olivia used a penlight she'd unearthed from a kitchen drawer to search the primary bedroom. Turning on any lights was too risky, since she had no way of knowing if the stalker was searching for them. The small flashlight was better than nothing, but the lack of illumination slowed her search.

The top of the dresser was free of clutter, each of the drawers cleaned out and ready for a guest to use. Susan and her husband, Mitch, rented the house for additional income, so it was pretty sparsely decorated. She searched through the nightstands and then moved to the closet. A few pieces of clothing hung in a far corner. Several shoeboxes were tucked underneath. Items Susan and Mitch had left for when they stayed in the cabin.

Olivia opened one, surprised to find lottery tickets tucked inside with a pair of women's sneakers. The next box was the same, except it contained a pair of hiking boots along with the lottery tickets. She knew Susan played, but not to this extent. There had to be hundreds of dollars in tickets here. Most of them were old though. Why keep them? Especially in the cabin that Susan didn't use often. It was strange but didn't help Olivia in the hunt for the satellite phone. She tossed the shoeboxes aside and scanned the space for a secret hiding place.

Nothing. Frustration bubbled. The only place left to look for the phone was in the bathroom. Grabbing the blanket off the bed, Olivia headed down the hall. It'd only been ten minutes since she left Cole, but worry plagued her. He was seriously injured. If they didn't find the phone soon, she'd have to leave him in the house and head back to the scene of the accident to get help.

Was the stalker still out there? She feared he was. Rain beat against the roof as another band of thunderstorms crossed their path. Any normal person would seek shelter from the harsh weather, but the man hunting them wasn't logical. He was on a mission. The cold and the rain wouldn't deter him.

Olivia slipped into the bathroom. Her heart skittered as panic shot through her like a bolt of lightning. "No, no, no."

Cole was slumped against the bathtub, his eyes closed. His complexion was ghostly pale in the weak beam of her penlight. Olivia couldn't tell if he was breathing. She dropped to her knees at his side and fumbled to feel for a pulse along the column of his throat. Tears blurred her vision.

An irregular and thready heartbeat thumped against her fingers. Olivia sucked in a breath. "Thank you, God."

Cole was alive, but the situation was more grave than ever. He needed help. Now.

She covered him with the blanket to help his body stay warm and then frantically searched the bathroom for the satellite phone. There was nothing in the cabinets but towels, washcloths, and small toiletries. The linen closet was locked though. Olivia fished the house keys out of her pocket, relieved to see a smaller key on the chain. She tried it in the lock and the door swung open.

Cleaning supplies neatly lined the shelves next to a few canned food items and extra water in case of an emergency. The satellite phone was plugged into an electrical outlet nestled in the back wall of the closet. Olivia snatched it up. Urgency ran through her as she dialed Eli's number. Praise sweet baby Jesus that she'd memorized his contact information, along with Cole's, when they took over the investigation.

Eli answered on the first ring. "Goodwin."

"It's Olivia. We crashed, and the stalker came after us. Cole and I escaped on foot and we're hiding at Susan's lake house." She quickly provided him the address before dropping to her knees and checking Cole's pulse. Still thready. "Cole's been shot. We need an ambulance ASAP. He's unconscious and has lost a lot of blood."

"Hold on." Eli's voice grew distant, but his barking tone indicated he was giving orders. Then his voice grew louder again. It sounded like he was running. "Police officers and EMS are en route. So am I. Help will be there in five minutes, Olivia. Just hang on."

Relief ran through her. The sound of glass shattering cut it short.

Olivia froze. "Eli, someone is breaking into the house."

They'd been found. Her stalker was here.

"Where are you in the house?" Eli barked. The roar of an engine punctuated his words, indicating he was in his vehicle. If he'd been at the scene of the accident, then he was less than five minutes away. Close. But not close enough. Her stalker was just down the hall.

"We're in the bathroom," Olivia whispered. She flipped the lock on the closed door, wincing at the noise it made. "I've locked the door, but it won't take him long to find us."

"Olivia..." The haunting voice sent a shiver down her spine. "Where are you? It's time, sweetheart. Time for us to be together."

Bile rose in the back of her throat. "He's here." She clutched the phone with one hand while taking the gun away from Cole with the other. The weight of the weapon was unfamiliar. Trembles coursed through her as she pointed the barrel at the door. "He's coming for me."

"Stay where you are."

Eli's command made sense. She was in a locked room and help was on the way, but the house wasn't big and the latch on the door was flimsy. Olivia knew it wouldn't take her stalker long to bust the door down. Her grandfather had taken her to the shooting range, but she didn't have any skills with a handgun. Nor could she rely on herself to fire under pressure. Taking a human life, even when the person was out to hurt her, didn't come naturally to Olivia.

"Sweetheart, come out, come out, wherever you are. There's not much time."

The sickening voice filtered under the door and twisted Olivia's insides. Cole groaned next to her. His life was on the line. If the stalker got into the bathroom, he'd murder Cole without batting an eye. But if Olivia ran... well, then her stalker would chase his prey and leave Cole alone.

It was a risk she had to take.

"He's getting too close," Olivia whispered to Eli. "I have to make a run for it to save Cole."

"Olivia, don't—"

His objection was cut off when she lowered the phone to the ground next to Cole. Eli called her name again, but she ignored him. Instead, she pressed a kiss to Cole's forehead. There was nothing she wouldn't do for this man. Nothing. He'd put his life on the line many times for her. Now it was her turn to be brave in order to save him.

Olivia rose and crossed to the bathroom door. She opened it and then re-latched the lock so it would engage when the door was shut. With a shuddering breath, and still gripping Cole's handgun, she slipped into the darkened hall.

A shape came out of the primary bedroom. A man, dressed in black, his face in shadows.

Olivia swallowed back a scream. She turned on her heel and ran for the door.

Her silent prayer was answered when the stalker raced down the hall after her. "Olivia, don't run, sweetheart."

She ignored him. Muscles bruised from the car accident protested as she bolted across the living room to the kitchen. The back door was open. Rain poured in, making the tiles slippery. Shattered glass crunched under Olivia's shoes from the busted pane in the top portion of the back door. She slid on a puddle and slammed her hip against the corner of a counter. Pain vibrated through her. She kept going, darting through the open doorway and into the full blast of the thunderstorm.

Lightning lit up the sky. Olivia dared a glance over her shoulder and caught sight of the stalker coming for her. He was several yards away, but closing fast. Raindrops pummeled her head as she spun and pulled the trigger on the gun. The blast shocked her, the recoil like a stiff kick to her arm.

The shot went wide. She didn't intend to hit him, or stop her attacker, only to give him a moment's pause. She was rewarded when he came to a screeching halt and ducked behind a tree. Before he could recover, she turned and ran for the tree line. The dense forest would be difficult to run through, but it could also provide thousands of hiding places. She prayed her stalker would use more caution in his approach now that he knew she was armed.

Was Cole okay? Was he still alive? Olivia was terrified his body wouldn't be able to cope with the blood loss he'd suffered. Or worse, what if he had an internal injury? The car accident had totaled his truck. Tears threatened to blind her as she ducked under a tree branch. Her feelings for Cole were much deeper than she'd allowed herself to acknowledge. Their shared kiss had proven that.

She'd lost so much. Her parents. Aaron. Would she also lose Cole?

God, please protect him. I know things will happen according to Your will, but I beseech you, please don't rip my heart out again. I love him and don't want to live my life without him.

Love. She did love Cole. There was no denying it. The spark that'd existed between them from their first meeting had grown into a powerful inferno fueled by friendship, respect, and unwavering trust.

Lightning lit up the sky again, illuminating the surrounding woods. Olivia had run parallel to the lake. Her breath came in pants and her muscles trembled with exhaustion. She didn't know how long she could keep going. Frigid air froze her wet clothes and hair to her skin. She paused, straining to listen for any sign of her stalker over the sound of the rain and her own pounding heart.

Her skin crawled. He was there. Close by. She could feel him.

A fresh wave of urgency put her feet in motion again. Thunder rumbled deep enough to vibrate through her chest. Olivia stumbled over a tree root, her hand shooting out to right herself. Another bolt of lightning blazed across the sky. She screamed.

The stalker was standing right in front of her.

TWENTY-SIX

Cole groaned. Every part of him hurt.

He pried his eyes open. A penlight illuminated the bathroom. He was still in Susan's house. A satellite phone rested next to him and his gun was gone. So was Olivia. Rain beat against the windows. Then a gunshot rang out.

Olivia! Cole willed his body to move, gritting his teeth against the sheer agony threatening to take him back into unconsciousness. Using the bathtub for support, he got himself into a standing position. The room spun for a moment but then settled down. His vision had cleared. The pain of his gunshot wound hadn't lessened, and it was still bleeding, but the bandage kept the worst of it at bay. He stumbled for the door.

Olivia was in danger. He had to save her.

If he could find her.

Please God, help me.

Fear shot through Olivia, freezing her in place, like a deer caught in the headlights.

Then the attacker lunged for her.

She raised the gun and shot at him. Again the bullet went wide, but this time, it didn't give him pause. He slammed into Olivia, knocking her backward. Her head rapped against the damp earth and the wind whooshed from her body as the stalker landed on top of her. The gun fell from her hand. It bounced out of reach under a bush.

Instinct and an embedded need to survive took over. Olivia scratched and clawed. She desperately tried to wriggle out from underneath the man trapping her. Air couldn't get into her lungs. Dots danced across her vision.

"Stop fighting me." He grabbed her wrist and tucked it underneath his powerful thigh.

Olivia attempted to use her other hand to gouge out his eye, but he reared back and then smacked her across the face. Pain exploded along her cheekbone. It momentarily stalled her movements, which gave him enough time to secure her other hand.

She was helpless.

He chuckled, leaning over her. Rain dripped from his hair onto her face. Darkness prevented her from making out all of his features, but she could see enough to confirm it was the man from the wedding. The waiter who'd drugged Jackson and Felicity. His high forehead led to beady, dark eyes, and a crooked mouth. Something about him was familiar, but she couldn't place where she knew him from. Maybe it was simply because she'd seen a photo of him in disguise just an hour ago.

"Who are you?" she wheezed. His weight on top of her prevented Olivia from fully inflating her lungs. "Did Justin send you?"

"All my secrets will be revealed in good time." He took her chin in his hand, studying her features with the gaze of a snake about to devour its meal. "For now, you can call me Master." He stroked her chin. "You are beautiful. I knew I had to have you from the moment I saw you."

She shuddered. "You sent me letters."

"Yes. Love letters." He twisted her head and leaned closer until he was inches from her face. Then something warm and wet scraped across her skin. His tongue. He was licking her cheek.

Bile rose in the back of Olivia's throat as disgust twisted her insides. She didn't know if Justin had hired this sicko, but one thing was certain: this man had stalked her in part because he was obsessed with her. And now she was trapped and at his mercy.

"This can be fun, if you let it." His breath was hot against the shell of her ear. "Say it. Say my name. Master."

He was disgusting. Olivia gagged and then gritted her teeth, refusing to give him the satisfaction. "You won't get away with this."

His hold on her chin tightened. He twisted her face until she was forced to look him in the eyes. They were dark recesses of evil. "Resisting me will only get you punished."

He was going to kill her anyway. Olivia had nothing to lose. She was fighting for her life, and knew it. This man holding her down thought she was weak. He was counting on it. But that wasn't the case. Olivia was brave. Cole had said so. Only hours ago, he told her she was the strongest person he knew. It was time to prove him right.

She head-butted her attacker. Agony ripped through her skull as her forehead collided with his nose. It crunched. Blood flew. He screamed like a baby and reared back enough for Olivia to wriggle her arms free. She closed her fist and punched him right in the apex of his thighs. He toppled to the side.

Chest heaving as she sucked in air, Olivia turned and scrambled to her feet. A hand shot out and grabbed her ankle. He yanked and she tumbled back down to the ground. Dirt and leaves broke her fall. In the next second, he was on her. His hands wrapped around her neck. Heart pounding, Olivia tried to jab him with her elbow. It didn't land. He bent her head back until she thought her spine would break, all the while squeezing her throat, cutting off her air supply.

"I told you not to fight me!"

He was unrelenting. Her body screamed for oxygen.

This was it. He was going to kill her.

A guttural cry came from the woods. Olivia caught sight of a dark shape one second before it collided with the man on top of her. The pressure on her neck disappeared.

Cole! Olivia wheezed, desperately trying to pull air into her aching lungs. The men rolled across the forest floor. The sound of flesh hitting flesh was punctuated by Cole's cry of pain. Olivia struggled to her feet and lunged for the gun hidden under the bush. Her hands only found dead leaves and twigs. Mud and water sank into the legs of her pantsuit.

Come on. Come on.

Finally her fingers brushed across metal. She yanked the gun free of the bush and turned, holding it in front of her. The men were locked in a deadly battle, but the stalker had gotten the upper hand. He was sitting on top of Cole. She pointed the barrel of the gun at him. "Stop or I will shoot you."

He lifted his head. Blood coated his nose and mouth. His lips curled into a sneer. "You don't have the nerve to shoot me."

Olivia's finger hovered over the trigger. It was him or Cole.

She chose Cole.

A calmness came over her. She was strong enough to protect the man she loved. Her gaze never wavered and determination hardened her tone. "Yes, I will."

"So will I." Eli emerged from the woods, gun drawn. "Get off him. Now. Then lay down on the ground with your hands on your head."

The stalker hesitated. Then more law enforcement officers came out of the trees. Several Texas Rangers—Grady and Bennett—were accompanied by Chief Sims and his officers. Every one of them had their guns pointed at the criminal. He wisely slid off Cole. There was a flurry of activity as he was searched and secured.

Olivia lowered her weapon and raced to Cole's side. He shoved against the damp ground into a sitting position. Then pulled her close with his good arm. "Are you hurt?" Cole pulled back to look her in the face. "Did he hurt you?"

Tears filmed her eyes. He was bleeding from a gunshot wound and had nearly died fighting with the attacker, but all he cared about was her injuries. She cupped his gorgeous mud-stained face and kissed him with all the passion inside her. Cole tightened his hold, bringing her closer. Her shelter in the storm.

She loved him. But how would Cole react when he found out?

Would he face his fears and try?

Or would he walk away?

TWENTY-SEVEN

A few days later, Cole eased into a sweater. It'd taken surgery and dozens of stitches to piece his shoulder back together. The bullet had torn through muscle, glanced off the bone, and just missed his brachial artery. He was lucky to be alive. While Cole was eternally grateful to the doctors and nurses who'd overseen his care, he was more than ready to bust out of the hospital. The food was terrible.

"Don't forget the sling." Jackson dangled the offending object in front of Cole.

He growled. "I don't need that."

"I'll call Nana back in here and tell her you refuse to listen to the doctors."

Cole's grandmother and Olivia were waiting in the hall while he dressed. The three of them hadn't left Cole's side since he came out of surgery. Nana fussed over him like he was ten years old. Olivia kept him occupied by reading books and watching sitcoms with him.

And Jackson...well, Jackson just annoyed him. Like a pesky younger brother.

Cole scowled at his fellow ranger. "Don't you have somewhere to be? You're on vacation. Go fish, or take a walk, or... I don't know. Whatever it is you do for fun."

"This is fun." Jackson extended the sling. "Put this on before I sic your grandmother on you." His mouth quirked. "She's the only woman I've ever seen successfully order you around. Except for Lieutenant Rodriguez... but she carries a gun."

Cole snorted and took the sling, grudgingly putting it on. The pressure on his wound eased, and he instantly felt better to his chagrin. "Nana doesn't order me around. She suggests. Strongly."

Jackson laughed. He'd recovered from being drugged with no lingering side effects. Their boss, Lieutenant Rodriguez, had ordered Jackson and Felicity to take some time for themselves. Instead of taking it easy, he was staking out Cole's hospital room, keeping an eye on him and Olivia.

Despite their banter, Cole appreciated his friend's presence. Although the man who'd stalked Olivia was in custody, there were a lot of unanswered questions about the case.

He crossed the room and opened the door. "I'm decent. You guys can come back in."

Nana entered first, her wide smile causing wrinkles to bunch around her dark eyes. She was a petite woman with a shock of white hair that contrasted with her olive skin. Knitting needles, ever present in her hands, were tucked against a ball of red yarn. "You look much better out of that hospital gown. There's color in your cheeks now." She patted his face. "A bit of homemade soup and some more rest, and you'll be back to normal."

He'd need more than homemade soup. The doctor warned it would take months of physical therapy to gain full mobility back. Then Cole would have to retrain with his firearm to make sure he was in top condition before returning to full duty. But that was a problem for another day.

Olivia followed Nana into the room. She wore a pair of white-washed jeans that hugged her hips and a flowy blouse that somehow made her eyes bluer than normal. Cole's breath hitched as her lips curved into a smile. The woman was stunning. In every way. He was tempted to lean forward and kiss her, but resisted. They hadn't had a moment alone to discuss their relationship.

"Special delivery from my grandparents." Olivia held up a tray of coffees. She set it on the bedside table and then handed one to Cole. "They stopped by to visit, but you were getting dressed. They'll come again after running some errands."

He took the coffee and drank. The rich brew instantly brightened his day. "Bless your grandparents. This was exactly what I needed."

Willie and Alyssa had come every day to see him. They'd brought food, changes of clothes, and asked their church friends to pray for him. They'd opened their home to Nana. She was currently sleeping in their guest room at night. They'd even arranged for home cooked meals to be delivered to the task force working the case. Cole could not imagine a more warm and generous couple.

"One of those is for me, right?" Jackson wiggled his eyebrows.

Olivia smiled. "Of course." She handed him a coffee. "One double-shot caramel macchiato with an extra dose of sugar."

Jackson kissed her cheek. "You're a doll."

The affection was brotherly, and although there was no logical reason to be jealous, Cole still felt a bolt of resentment shoot through him. Jackson's interactions with Olivia were effortless, while he felt like he was walking on eggshells. A prison of his own making. Cole wasn't sure he was ready to face how deep his feelings for Olivia were.

Nana studied him from the chair next to the bed. Her knitting needles flowed without missing a stitch, but he felt the weight of her assessment. Cole ignored her pointed look and took another sip of his coffee. "The doctor says I'll be released this afternoon."

Olivia's smile widened. "That's great news." Her expression was filled with so much warmth it made his chest ache. "My grandparents told me you are more than welcome to stay with them for a while. Just until you're back on your feet and have better use of your arm."

"That sounds like an excellent idea." Nana's knitting needles clacked. "We accept."

"Nana..." Cole stared, trying to convey everything he wanted to say with just a look.

This time, she ignored him. "It makes common sense, Cole. You need rest and you'll have to do a follow-up visit with the doctor in a few days anyway. Not to mention you have your truck to handle. It won't hurt to accept the Leightons' generous offer of hospitality."

She was right, but Cole worried that more time with Olivia would simply make it impossible to leave. And he wasn't certain he could stay. There were so many considerations, first and foremost, her wellbeing.

Was he destined to follow in his parents' footsteps? To make their mistakes? He hadn't had the ability to sort any of that out, and the last thing Cole wanted was to lead Olivia on.

A knock interrupted their conversation. Cole turned just as Eli and Chief Sims entered. Both men looked exhausted. Eli's chin was peppered with a five-o'clock shadow and the chief's clothes were rumpled. It looked like they'd been up for hours, even though it was eight a.m.

"Sorry to disturb you folks." Chief Sims lifted his cowboy hat in greeting to Olivia and then Nana before turning to Cole. "We've got an update on the case to discuss with you and Olivia, if you don't mind."

"Nana, why don't you and I get some breakfast in the cafeteria?" Jackson offered his arm to the older woman and escorted her from the room. He closed the door behind them.

Olivia came to stand next to Cole. He instantly took her hand in a gesture of support. Her muscles were stiff, but they relaxed at his touch. She interlaced their fingers.

"We've got good news and bad news." Chief Sims settled one hand on his duty belt. The leather creaked. "The good news is that the man who attacked you in the woods has been identified as Bryce McDonnell. He's got a rap sheet going back to his teen years that includes stalking and harassing women. In early 2001, he was charged with the murder of a woman in Magnolia and did twenty-three years in prison. He was released two months ago."

Astonished, Cole arched his brows. "That's the good news?"

"Yeah. The bad news is that he lawyered up and is refusing to talk. His bond request was denied seeing as we caught him actually attacking Olivia, so he'll be rotting away in jail until the trial." The chief focused on Olivia and his expression grew sympathetic. "Unless he makes a deal with the prosecutor, you'll have to testify."

"I'll do whatever is necessary to make sure justice is served." Her gaze skipped to Eli. "Is Bryce connected to Justin?"

"We're still tracking that down. The men were in prison together and housed in the same unit, so we know they crossed paths. We can't confirm that Justin hired Bryce to stalk you though."

"It appears he was working alone however," Chief Sims added. "We've been through his cell phone and tracked his movements since he came to Serenity. There's no sign Bryce had a partner. He's solely responsible for the notes, the break-ins at your house, and all the attacks."

Cole frowned. "How do you explain the stolen jewelry?"

The chief shrugged. "Bryce needed cash. He was staying at a cheap motel about an hour away and the rent was due."

That made sense, but something about this felt too neatly tied up. "How did he always know where to find Olivia? I never spotted him following us. Plus, the stalker knew a lot about Serenity. Which stores had cameras and so forth. How did Bryce manage that? Does he have a tie to someone in town?"

"Not that we've uncovered, but Bryce got very good at stalking. He's been doing it for a long time, and after getting caught for murder, I'm sure he learned a few more tricks from the other prisoners in jail." The chief rocked back on his heels. "We'll continue to work the case, but I think it's safe to say this is all over."

"Well, that's a relief." Olivia breathed out.

Chief Sims nodded. "I'm sure it is." He opened the tablet in his hand. "I've written up your statement, Olivia. Would you mind reviewing it? I'll also need your signature."

"Of course."

Cole tilted his head to show Eli should join him on the other side of the room next to the window. He pitched his voice low to keep the chief from overhearing. "Are you in agreement with Chief Sims?"

"Mostly. It's true there's no sign Bryce was working with anyone else. We searched his hotel room and found numerous disguises. Once we knew what they were, a review of the surveillance videos at Oak Gardens confirmed he was there, scoping out the place days before the chandelier attack. This is also probably why you never spotted him following you. The disguises were good ones. Prosthetic noses and ears, high-quality wigs, that kind of thing. I also think that's how he got close enough to deliver the notes to Olivia without her noticing him. He never looked the same."

That eased some of Cole's concerns. "How was he getting around town? He had to have a car."

"Multiple. Bryce knows a man who owns a dealership. The guy would let him borrow different cars and then bring them back when he was done. These attacks on Olivia were well-planned." Eli rubbed the back of his neck. "Bryce had a long time to think about how he was going to do this. Which brings us back to Justin. Did they plan it while in prison together? I don't want to close this case until we know the answer to that."

"What about Justin's girlfriend, Caroline? The one who withdrew the money from his account?"

"We can't find her. I suspect Bryce killed her after getting the money, but I can't prove it. Not yet. I'm coordinating with the District Attorney in the hopes that we can come to some sort of plea bargain. It'll require Bryce to explain everything he did and reveal anyone else's involvement." Eli's mouth hardened. "If he did murder Caroline, I want to know where her body is. Her family deserves that closure."

Cole agreed. Plea bargains were a common occurrence. This crime was heinous and Texas had the death penalty. Criminals often agreed to a lesser charge of life in prison without the possibility of parole. Bryce had been caught trying to outright kill Olivia. He had little bargaining power at this point. He also wasn't stupid. Chances were, Bryce and his lawyer were already coming up with an offer for the District Attorney.

Additionally, if he admitted his guilt, it would save Olivia from having to testify. She'd already been through so much, and although she would do what was necessary, Cole hoped it wouldn't come to that.

Eli slapped Cole lightly on the back of his uninjured shoulder. "Don't look so worried. I've got this."

"I know you do." Cole trusted him implicitly but couldn't shake the feeling that something wasn't right.

He prayed he was wrong.

For Olivia's sake.

TWENTY-EIGHT

After Eli and Chief Sims left, Olivia opened the cover on Cole's breakfast. Scrambled eggs, toast, and some grits. None of it looked appetizing. She wrinkled her nose. "Maybe you should ask Nana to bring you some food from the cafeteria."

Cole chuckled as he eased onto the edge of the bed. "It's a step up from what they were serving me right after surgery. Although I won't complain if your grandmother makes her famous meatloaf for dinner."

"She'll be happy to." Olivia pushed the tray over to the bed so Cole could eat. "Do you need any pain medicine?" She checked her watch. It'd been hours since his last dose. "The nurse said you could ask for more—"

Cole pushed away the tray of food and snagged her hand in his. His warm touch sent a bolt of heat straight through her. "You don't need to fuss over me. I can manage." His mouth quirked. "Besides, that's Nana's job."

Her cheeks heated. "I don't mean to suggest you can't..." Olivia licked her lips and pulled her hand away. She'd never asked Cole if her presence was bothersome. Maybe she should have, but gosh, it hurt to think he didn't want her there. "I'm just trying to help. I'm sorry if I've upset you."

"You haven't upset me in the least." Cole shook his head in frustration, rising from the bed to stop her from moving away from him. "I'm sorry. I think my comment came out wrong. You've been at my side day and night. I'm worried about you exhausting yourself, especially after everything that happened." He gently cupped her face. "You need rest too. Time to decompress."

There he was, taking care of her again. Olivia still wasn't used to it. She stepped forward and wrapped her arms around his waist. Cole embraced her with his usable arm, pulling her close. Careful not to jostle his wound, she laid her head on his chest and took a deep breath. "This feels pretty calming to me."

His mouth brushed against the top of her head. The move was tender and loving. It brought tears to Olivia's eyes. Since the shooting, she'd been running on adrenaline and caffeine. Every ounce of her energy had been poured into making sure Cole was comfortable and recovering. But he was right. She hadn't taken a moment to process everything that happened. The safety of his embrace allowed the wall surrounding her emotions to crack open.

The steady beat of his heart thumped against her ear.

Olivia was grateful he was okay. "You nearly died, Cole. I was so scared."

"So was I." His hold tightened around her waist. "When I woke up in that bathroom and you weren't there. Then the gunshot...." Cole pulled back until they were looking each other in the face. "Jackson told me what you did by running out of the bathroom to prevent Bryce from finding me. You put your life on the line to save mine. There are no words to express what I feel."

She didn't need words. Everything was there in the depths of his brown eyes. Gratitude and admiration. Maybe even love.

Olivia's breath hitched. She rose up on her tiptoes to brush a kiss across his mouth. Cole closed his eyes, and for a moment, she thought he would deepen the kiss, but then he leaned his forehead against hers.

"I care about you, Olivia. So much. But nothing has changed since our last conversation. A relationship... marriage... it's not for me." He pulled away, stepping out of her embrace. "I don't want to lead you on."

"You aren't." Olivia wrapped her arms around her midsection to ward off the cold air that had rushed into the space between them. A part of her wanted to turn tail and run away from this conversation, but she refused to do it. This moment required bravery. A different kind than the one she'd used when escaping a killer in the woods, but no less intense, as it demanded she expose her heart in a way she'd never done before.

"In fact, you've been very honest about your feelings on the matter." Olivia sucked in a steadying breath and then squared her shoulders before lifting her gaze to meet his. "So allow me to be upfront with you. I'm in love with you, Cole."

He inhaled sharply, his eyes widening at the bluntness of her statement. She let the words hang in the air between them for several seconds before continuing, "I fought against these feelings. I've been brokenhearted before. Aaron's death was difficult for me to get through. I never thought I'd find love again and then you came along. From the moment we met, there was something special between us. I did my best to keep you at arm's length, but it was impossible.

"You've protected and cared for me. Given me a safe space to share my feelings and my problems. You've supported me through one of the hardest times of my life..." Tears filmed her eyes again as emotions flooded through her. "You've been my friend, and every time you touch me, Cole, I light up inside. It's not a fluke or misguided appreciation. It's love. I adore your smile. The way your eyes crinkle when you laugh. How deep your faith runs. The way you take care of everyone around you, including your friends, and the amazing way you speak about your grandmother."

He didn't say a word. Cole stood there, stock still, as if he was in shock. But he didn't interrupt her or tell her to stop. He was listening to every word, and that gave Olivia the confidence to continue.

"I know you're scared of following in your parents' footsteps, but I believe in us. In what we can build together, with God as our guide. Things can be different,

Cole, but you have to choose it. You have to work for it." Olivia sucked in a shuddering breath. "I love you with all my heart. I know you may still walk away from us, and if that's the case, I'll be okay. But you should know exactly what you're rejecting. You deserved to know the truth about my feelings. Think it over. Whatever you decide, I'll respect it."

Silence descended in the room. Cole opened his mouth and then closed it. Olivia sensed his confusion and turmoil. She didn't want to make this worse for him. The point was to be honest with her feelings and then give him the space to decide.

Her heart also hurt. It was romantic and foolish, but a small part of her hoped he'd echo her feelings. She needed her own time and space. "I'm starving. I'll join your grandmother and Jackson in the cafeteria."

Olivia spun on her heel and walked out of the room, closing the door behind her. The tears filming her eyes fell onto her cheeks. She swiped them away. No matter what happened, she was proud of herself for being brave. There was nothing else to be done now. The ball was in Cole's court.

She took another breath to steady her emotions and then walked to the elevator. A beep came from her cell phone. Her grandparents had bought her a new one the day after the accident. Olivia pulled it from her pocket and checked the text message. It was from David.

I'm so sorry about what happened the other night. Can we meet at your office this morning so I can apologize in person? I feel terrible about what happened and would like the opportunity to explain.

Olivia hesitated for a moment, fear creeping along her spine, but then she gave herself a mental shake. Chief Sims and Eli said Bryce was working alone. David's behavior the other night was weird, but stress had caused her to misinterpret his actions as hostile. It was better to clear the air sooner, rather than later. Grandpa had left his truck for her to use in the hospital parking lot. She could pop to the office, have a discussion with David, and check on a few things for Eli and Sienna's wedding.

Decision made, she texted David. The elevator doors swung open and Olivia stepped out onto the ground floor. Instead of heading toward the cafeteria, she turned left for the parking lot. As she stepped into the brilliant sunny day, a silent whisper of doubt caused her to hesitate once more. She glanced back at the hospital doors. It felt weird to be going somewhere alone. She hadn't done it in over a week.

But the danger was over. It was time to reclaim her life.

Olivia crossed the lot toward the truck.

TWENTY-NINE

Cole hung his head in his hands. It'd been twenty minutes since Olivia left his hospital room and his mind was still spinning with everything she'd said. A part of him wanted to jump for joy, the other part of him wanted to run and never stop, and a third wanted to cry. He couldn't untangle the knot of emotions lodged in his chest. Everything was a mess.

And it was all his fault.

"Cole?" A gentle hand touched the top of his head. "Are you all right, honey?"

Nana. He hadn't even heard her come in. Cole lifted his head to find his grandmother standing at his side. Jackson was nowhere to be seen. Neither was Olivia. They must still be in the cafeteria. Cole wouldn't blame Olivia if she never spoke to him again. She'd poured her heart out, said some of the most touching things he'd ever heard in his life, and he'd stood there like a dunce.

She hadn't deserved that, but he'd been at a loss for

words. The internal war inside him had left him adrift in confusion. He'd prayed, but it didn't feel like God was interested in answering at the moment.

"Olivia's in love with me." Cole hadn't intentionally meant to say the words out loud, but once he did, relief washed over him. If anyone could understand what he was going through, it was Nana.

"Well, that's obvious to anyone with eyes." She settled on the window seat next to him. Her hand slipped into the pocket of her dress and she removed her rosary beads. "And I know you're in love with her too, so I'm confused about where the problem is."

"I'm not built for marriage. I'm too much like my parents and I don't want to make the same mistake they did. My temper lurks under the surface. I can feel it. It's only a matter of time before it comes out again and destroys everything." Pain tore his heart in two. "Just like it did on the night my parents died."

"Cole..." Nana rubbed his back like he was five years old, crying on her lap about a busted knee. "What happened that night wasn't your fault. Your parents are responsible for their decisions. It was their job to protect you. Instead, they trapped you in a car and made you listen to more yelling and screaming than anyone has a right to hear, let alone a little boy."

Heat built behind his eyes. Intellectually, he understood what his grandmother was saying, but it was hard to let go of the guilt. "If I hadn't screamed—"

"They might've had the accident anyway. It wasn't the first one."

He inhaled sharply and turned to face his grandmother. "What?"

"Your mother and father had a prior car accident, about a year before they died. Totaled their car." She clutched her rosary. "Your mom was in the hospital for a week. It was caused by them fighting."

"I didn't know about that."

Nana shook her head, her mouth taut. "It happened in the summer while you were staying with me. I didn't say anything because I didn't want you to worry." She sighed, suddenly looking weary. "I've tried to protect you but haven't done a good job."

"That's not—"

"It's true. Before your parents died, I tried to convince them to let you live with me. They refused. I didn't fight them on it. That was my first mistake. My second has been keeping the truth about their relationship from you." She tangled her hands together in her lap, the rosary wrapped around her gnarled fingers. "Cole, your parents were never a good match from the start. They were both young and too immature to get married."

He frowned. "Are you saying they didn't love each other?"

"Maybe they did, but it was a toxic situation. Jealousy, anger, accusations, and drama were the foundation of their marriage. Not love. Not the kind of lasting affection, trust, and loyalty needed to make a long-term relationship work. It was doomed to fail before it even started. Then they got pregnant with you." Nana gazed at him with warmth. "I thank God for you every day, but I'll admit that I cried the day my son told me he was going to be a father. The situation between your parents... it was no place for a child."

Something inside Cole twisted hard. He knew Nana loved him deeply, but she was right. The household he grew up in had been a war zone. It wasn't any place for a child, and it was validating to hear someone else acknowledge how awful it had been. "Did they ever love me?"

"They did." She took his hand in hers. "But they were so wrapped up in controlling each other, neither bothered to take care of your needs. I'm so sorry, sweetheart. I should've fought harder to get you out of that situation. Your dad threatened to keep you away from me for good, and the lawyers didn't think I would win a custody fight, so I played along."

"You have nothing to apologize for."

His parents could act properly in public. His dad was a successful carpenter and his mom had worked in a hotel. They'd had friends and knew how to be charming. It was only in the privacy of their home that the masks came off and their actual feelings came out.

Back then, emotional abuse wasn't spoken about, and grandparents didn't have the right to visitation in Texas. Nana had done the right thing by staying quiet. "The summers I spent with you were some of my happiest times."

"They were some of mine too. I wish... I wish your grandfather had lived long enough to help raise you. Walter was the best thing that ever happened to me." She squeezed his hand. "Not all marriages are like your parents. Walter and I had decades of happiness together. He was my best friend, and even though losing him broke my heart, I wouldn't have traded the time we spent together for anything in the world."

"I know sometimes it works out. Many of the rangers on my team are happily married." Secretly, Cole wanted that for himself, but not just with anyone. With Olivia. "But how do you know if it'll last? Some people are in love when they get married, but still end up divorced."

"That's true. But Cole, love isn't just a feeling, it's an action. A thousand small decisions made every day. You choose to compromise, to listen, and to grow together. It's about facing life's challenges together with respect and consideration for each other. Walter and I didn't always see eye to eye, but we talked through our differences until we found a solution that worked for both of us. You can't predict the future, but you can commit to make the choice to fight for your love every day."

His grandmother's words echoed Olivia's. *You have to choose it. You have to work for it.* Cole let those words finally sink into his soul, let them wash away the hurt of the past so he could see a future that was happy. One full of love. "Olivia essentially told me the same thing. That with work, and God as our guide, we can build something together."

"She's a smart woman." Nana grinned. "You didn't ask, but I'll say it anyway. Olivia is someone who will stand by you when things get hard. She risked her life to save yours, just like you did to save hers. That's the kind of selflessness and courage that forms the basis for a lasting relationship. You two have already proven you can support each other through hard times. So if you love her, then I recommend you tell her. And hold on tight. She's worth it."

Olivia was absolutely worth it. He couldn't wait to talk to her.

Cole rose from the window seat and kissed his grandmother on the head. "Thank you, Nana."

She beamed at him, the light from the window hitting on the cross attached to her rosary. It struck Cole then, in that moment, that God had heard his prayers. And answered them. He'd sent Nana to advise him with her words of wisdom.

No. It was more than that. The good Lord had been listening all along. Not to the words coming from Cole's mouth, but to the cries of his heart. For love and happiness. For someone to share his life with. He'd sent Olivia, the perfect partner for Cole, a brave woman who'd pushed him to face his fears and embrace the love they could have together.

What had he told Olivia? Their relationship was divinely guided. The incidents pushing them together were too perfectly aligned to be anything but the good Lord's handiwork. At the time, Cole believed it was so he could protect Olivia from the stalker. And that had been part of it. But God had a bigger plan.

I'm following, Lord. Lead me and I will follow. And thank you. For everything.

The phone at Cole's bedside rang. He'd been fielding

calls from friends for the last two days. He picked up the receiver. "Donnelly."

"Cole, it's Eli. Where's Olivia?"

His tone was clipped and controlled, but there was an underlying urgency that sent Cole's heart rate spiking. "She's in the cafeteria with Jackson."

"No, she isn't."

Cole whirled to face his grandmother. "What do you mean? She left forty-five minutes ago to join you and Jackson for breakfast."

Nana's eyes were wide as she registered the panic in his expression. "She never showed up there. Jackson saw a friend he went to college with, so I left him in the cafeteria and came back up here. Olivia wasn't with him when I left. Is it possible I missed her somehow?"

At that moment, Jackson strolled into the hospital room. He took one look at Cole's expression and the smile instantly fled his lips. "What is it?"

"Olivia's not with you?"

"No. I thought she was with you."

"We need to find her." Eli had obviously overheard the entire conversation. "ASAP. Bryce just admitted in questioning that he wasn't working alone, but he won't tell us who his accomplice is without a firm plea bargain in place. The District Attorney is hashing out the details, but if Olivia is missing, that changes everything."

It sure did.

Olivia was still in danger.

THIRTY

The bells over the door jingled as Olivia stepped into her office. The scent of coffee and fresh pastries tickled her nose and brought a smile to her face. Her stomach growled. Susan's chair was empty, but her purse and keys rested on the desk. Romantic piano music played from the Bluetooth speaker.

Olivia beelined for the break room. "I'm here, Susan."

The pipes rattled overhead and she realized her secretary was in the bathroom. Olivia poured herself a cup of coffee, topping it off with a generous helping of hazelnut creamer. Then she nosed around in the pastry box on the table. A blueberry muffin was on top. Cole's favorite.

A pang hit her heart. Olivia would miss having him in the office. He'd been a terrible assistant—no creativity at all—but his kindness and their fun banter more than made up for it. Scratch that. She'd miss Cole. A part of her heart was hoping that he'd change his mind about their relationship, but she knew the chances were slim. He'd been very honest with her from the beginning about marriage, love, and the whole she-bang. She'd chosen to ignore him. But no matter how this went, she didn't regret falling in love with him.

He'd shown her what was possible. Olivia wouldn't settle for anything less than fireworks, steadfast support, and a man she could trust with her life.

She sighed, choosing a bear claw from the box, and then promised to come back for the chocolate scone. Caffeine and sugar were the best remedies at the moment. And work. Excitement added a bounce to her steps as she crossed the lobby to her office. Nothing made her happier than finalizing a wedding. Eli and Sienna wanted something simple, but she'd added a few details to make it special all the same.

Using a napkin as a makeshift plate, Olivia set the bear claw down on her desk. She flipped open her laptop to power it on and then, coffee in hand, she dug through the mood boards leaning against the wall until she found the right one. Eli and Sienna's colors were navy and cream, with touches of brown to add a rustic feel.

A thump came from the closet. Olivia froze. What on earth was that? Had something fallen? The closet held office supplies and a few odds and ends. It would be awful if a shelf had broken. She reached for the doorknob and then paused. Some whispered instinct caused the hair on the back of her neck to rise.

Another thump came from inside the closet.

Her heart skipped a beat and then took off. Coffee sloshed over the edge of her mug, burning the skin on her hand. She barely felt it. If there was an animal inside the closet—like a raccoon or an opossum—she was going to have a heart attack. With a bracing grimace, she twisted the doorknob and jumped back.

Shock and horror flooded through her. It wasn't a raccoon in the closet.

"David!"

He'd been beaten and tied to a chair. Silver tape locked his mouth shut. Olivia took one step toward him, intent on releasing his bonds. His eyes widened as he caught sight of something behind her. She whirled.

Susan stood a few feet away. She had the barrel of a gun pointed straight at Olivia's chest. "Don't move. Not one more step."

Confusion and fear mingled with the shock and horror of finding David in the closet. Olivia stared incredulously at her secretary. "What are you doing?"

Susan smirked. "Solving a problem. Actually, multiple problems."

Olivia's gaze flickered to the lobby. It was dark, as if they weren't there, and the blinds were drawn.

Susan chuckled. "I locked the door, put on the closed sign, and turned out the lights. No one is coming to rescue you, boss. Not this time."

She was on her own. Olivia clutched the cup of coffee in her hand until her knuckles were white. "I don't understand. Why are you doing this?"

"Why else? Money." Susan sneered. "My husband

and I are broke. We're going to lose the lake house next month."

With a jolt of understanding, Olivia stiffened. All the lottery tickets in the lake house suddenly made sense. Susan had complained her husband wasn't working steadily even before Mitch injured his back. They'd been struggling for a while.

Olivia had given Susan a raise. Clearly, that wasn't enough. Susan had a gambling problem and had likely squandered away the extra money. "Justin hired you, along with Bryce."

"Bryce is a distant cousin of mine. He and Justin were in prison together and got to talking, realized they knew many of the same people. Like me. I guess over time Justin showed Bryce photos of you and he became obsessed." Her mouth pursed as if she'd sucked on something sour. "Bryce was always weird. But when he got out of prison and offered me a lot of money to feed him information, I immediately accepted."

"Did you know he intended to kill me?"

She shrugged. "I didn't think about it. Easier that way."

Olivia was sure. "They needed someone who knew my schedule so Bryce could follow me." Cole had been right to question the chief about that. Olivia wished she could tell him that. "What else did they pay you for?"

"Just information at first. Where the cameras in town were, what your schedule was. And then things got interesting when Mitch had to break into your house and leave a note on the bed."

Shock vibrated through Olivia. She remembered thinking the intruder on the camera footage seemed familiar. Now she knew why. It'd been Susan's husband. "He stole some of my jewelry."

"We needed cash." She waved the gun. "This is the weapon he shot at Cole with. Once Justin confirms that he's transferred the additional fifty grand we've asked for, I'll use this gun to shoot you. Then David. It'll look like the perfect murder-suicide."

Olivia couldn't believe her ears. "No one will believe that. David's clearly been beaten."

"Yeah, Mitch should've been more gentle with him." Susan shrugged. "It doesn't matter. You did a number on Bryce before the police caught him. I'll make it look like there was a struggle."

"Where is Mitch now?" She scanned the immediate area, discreetly looking for some kind of weapon. There was nothing.

"He's driving back from the prison. We had to pay a hefty bribe to a guard in order to get Justin a cell phone, so he has access to his bank account. Once he transfers the money that was promised, I'm going to video chat with him so he can watch you die."

She wasn't bluffing. Susan's expression had turned into one of cold-blooded hatred. Olivia couldn't compute how the woman she'd worked next to for the last three years was hiding such a twisted dark side. She really was naïve. Or maybe desperation and panic had turned Susan into someone else.

Olivia stepped forward, still clutching the coffee

mug. "You don't have to do this. It's not too late to change your mind." She swallowed hard. "Susan... please... I thought we were friends."

"We were until you hired David!" Susan's outburst was violent and unexpected. Her face turned bright red with rage. "Then things changed. I hated him and asked you to fire him, but you wouldn't listen." She jabbed the gun in Olivia's direction. "You did this. It's all your fault."

Like flipping a switch, Susan's anger turned to sadness. She tucked a few loose curls behind her ears and then smoothed her blouse. "I'm sorry, Olivia, but this is how it has to be. I need the money." Her expression turned beseeching. "It won't hurt. I promise. And I tried to keep David out of it. If you hadn't fought so hard, and Bryce had killed you, then none of this would've happened. I had to go to Plan B. It's really all your fault, don't you see?"

Unbelievable. Olivia was absolutely disgusted, but she took another step toward Susan. The only chance she had for survival was to get the gun away from the other woman. "I understand. This is an impossible situation. You have no choice." She scooted closer. "There's just one thing I don't understand. When Cole and I asked you about David's involvement, you denied it. If the plan was to frame him, then why tell us that?"

"Jeez, you really are slow. Listen, Olivia. Back then, that wasn't the plan. I was paid only to provide information to Bryce. He delivered the notes and followed you around. I kept him advised of what I knew about the case from the police, which he also paid me for. Then he needed Mitch to break into your house, so we upped our ask, and we upped it again when he asked me to find out everything I could about Cole." Her gaze narrowed. "I didn't expect you to have a Texas Ranger following you around. That complicated matters. When you and Cole asked about David, I simply wanted to muddy the waters of the investigation to protect Bryce and myself."

"That's why you implicated Randy. Smart."

"Exactly." Susan beamed like a child being praised for solving a tough math problem. "Bryce was supposed to kill you and Cole, but he screwed up. That's when Mitch and I figured we could make Justin a new deal. Problem was, we needed someone to pin the murder on. That's where David comes in. Everyone's heard about the incident the other night at Oak Gardens. It's not a stretch to believe he was working with Bryce."

Susan's cell phone rang, interrupting their conversation. The screen lit up with an unknown number. It was Justin.

Olivia was out of time.

She threw the coffee in her mug at Susan. The woman recoiled and instinctively put her hands up to protect her face. She yelped as the still-hot liquid scalded her skin. Olivia tossed the mug at her head for good measure and then lunged for the gun.

She wrapped her fingers around the metal, but Susan was stronger than she looked. She wouldn't let go. Olivia twisted, trying to get the upper hand, as Susan grabbed a fistful of her hair and yanked. Pain erupted in her scalp, but she kept trying to get the gun away. Her heart thundered against her ribcage. She stomped on Susan's foot.

Glass shattered in the lobby. Olivia heard Cole shout her name.

Then the gun in her hands went off.

THIRTY-ONE

Red and blue lights flashed across the sidewalk in stark contrast to the otherwise sunny day. Police officers, Texas Rangers, and EMS swarmed Olivia's office. She'd brushed off any offer of medical assistance, content to take shelter in Cole's loving embrace. His arm was wrapped around her waist and she leaned into him as two paramedics hurried past with a gurney. Susan was handcuffed to the rail, screaming defenses and nonsense, the leg of her jeans bloody. The bullet had struck her in the calf when the gun went off.

Susan spotted Olivia and started spewing obscenities. The hatred pouring from her was like a physical slap, and although Olivia knew she couldn't hurt her anymore, it still stung.

She turned her face away. "I can't believe I ever considered her a friend."

"You're a kind, warm, generous woman." Cole gently

lifted her chin until she was staring into his eyes. "Never apologize for believing in the best of people. It's a strength, not a weakness. And it's one of the things I love about you."

Her heart skipped several beats, and she blinked, certain she hadn't heard him correctly. "What did you say?"

"I love you, Olivia. With all my heart. I'm sorry I didn't say it earlier. I was scared, but Nana gave me a good talking to and set me right."

"I knew I liked her."

Cole chuckled. "And she adores you." His thumb gently caressed the curve of her chin, sending butterflies alighting in her belly. "My feelings for you are so deep and powerful... it terrified me. I've faced down deadly criminals, put myself in the line of fire, but when it came to dealing with what was happening between us, I was a coward. I tried to run from it."

She'd figured that part out. "That's why you didn't want to be my bodyguard when Eli and Sienna suggested it."

He nodded. "Then I tried to box it up. I kept talking about how much I don't want to get married, hoping it would put up a wall between us. Nothing worked. What I felt for you kept growing until there was no way to deny it." Cole's gaze dropped to her lips. "And then you kissed me and my entire world went topsy-turvy. I've told myself for so long that I didn't need love. Not this kind, anyway. But you smashed through all my excuses. It took time, prayer, and a conversation with Nana, but I finally got my head on right."

He brushed a kiss across her mouth. "My past doesn't define me, just like you said. I decide who I want to be."

Her heart swelled, and she lifted her hands to rest on his neck. "Yes, you do. And for the record, I think you're fantastic."

"Ditto, sweetheart." He lightly kissed her again. "We can build a future together, with God as our guide. I believe in us too." A flicker of doubt creased his features, and he hesitated. "Unless you've changed your mind."

She placed a finger over his lips to shush him. "Never."

A throat cleared, interrupting their intimate conversation. Olivia turned her head to see David standing a few feet away. His shirt was stained with blood and he held an ice pack up to his cheekbone.

"Sorry to interrupt, but I wanted to thank you both." David drew closer, lowering the ice pack. "You saved my life."

During Olivia's fight with Susan, Cole and several Serenity police officers arrived. They heard a scream and subsequently broke into the office through one of the windows, arriving in the nick of time. Bryce was currently being interviewed by the District Attorney, Chief Sims, and Eli. He was telling them everything now that Susan was in custody. Mitch had already been arrested by state troopers. Cole had assured Olivia everyone involved would go to prison for a long time.

"I'm sorry you got dragged into this." Olivia felt horrible that her former assistant had almost been killed. David must've been terrified. "Did Susan convince you to come to the office this morning?"

"No. Last night. I contacted her after being questioned by the rangers at Oak Gardens, and she confirmed you were being stalked. I realized that's why you panicked when I asked you to dinner." His expression turned remorseful. "I'm so sorry, Olivia. I can see now that I frightened you, but please believe me, that wasn't my intention."

"I know." She'd been overly cautious after the attacks. Thinking back on the interaction, David hadn't done anything overtly threatening. Under normal circumstances, she wouldn't have thought anything of it.

"Anyway last night, Susan said you would be in the office and explained I could stop by to discuss the issue with you. When I arrived, I was attacked by Mitch. He tied me up and stuck me in the closet. I was there all night. In the morning, Susan took my phone, unlocked it, and sent a text message to you. When I heard you come in, I started banging on the floor to get your attention, hoping you'd be able to escape before Susan attacked you."

Olivia's heart sank to her feet. She felt horribly guilty about suspecting David. "You tried to save my life."

"Friends take care of each other." David met her gaze. "That's all I've ever felt for you, Olivia. Friendship. My heart belongs to Angie. We've had a really hard time lately, but I'm determined to get us back on track. Being tied up and locked in a closet gave me a lot of time to think about my mistakes."

A flash of color caught Olivia's attention over David's shoulder. She recognized the pretty woman in the red sweatshirt. Panic was written all over her features as she went from police officer to police officer, trying to get past the crime scene tape.

Olivia pointed. "David, Angie's here. Now might be a good time to start correcting those mistakes."

His expression froze, and then he turned on his heel. The moment David saw Angie, he sprinted across the distance between them. The couple embraced in a fierce hug and Angie began crying. David kissed her.

Watching them, Olivia's heart swelled. "I hope they can work things out."

"So do I."

She turned to face Cole, rising to brush a kiss across his lips. A thrill went through her, and she was tempted to deepen the kiss, but they were in public. "Well, Ranger Donnelly, now that all the people responsible for stalking me are in custody, what do you say we have our official first date? I skipped breakfast, and having my life threatened really leaves a girl hungry."

"Sure. On one condition."

She leaned back, eyeing him suspiciously. "What is it?"

"You help me write my speech for Eli's wedding." He grinned. "It's in a few days and I still don't know what I'm going to say."

She laughed. "I can do that."

He rubbed his nose against hers, stalling her breath. "We make a good team, Olivia. I love you."

"I love you too."

THIRTY-TWO

Nerves jittered Cole's insides. He tugged on the tie threatening to cut off his air supply. The temperatures inside the rustic barn were cool, but sweat still beaded along his forehead. In a few minutes, he was going to be standing in front of a crowd, many of them people he worked with and saw regularly. If he screwed this up, it was going to be humiliating. Worse, he'd let down Eli and Sienna.

"Stop fidgeting." Olivia stepped in front of him, set her clipboard down, and then straightened his tie. Then she put her hands on his biceps. "You've got this."

"Yeah, Donnelly." Jackson waggled his brows. "Don't worry about the videographer. I'm sure they can cut you out if they need to."

Some more of the blood drained from his face. "Videographer..."

"Stop it." Olivia gave Jackson a light shove. "You're not helping, and if you don't act supportive, I'm going to put you on valet duty. You'll spend the rest of the wedding fetching people's cars. Or worse." Her eyes widened with a sudden idea. "You'll be on clean-up and gift delivery duty. Last wedding I did, it took three trips to deliver everything to the bride's house."

"Okay, okay. No need to threaten me." Jackson held up his hands in mock surrender. "I'm just having some fun." He glanced in Cole's direction and grimaced slightly. "Come to think of it, you look pale." He clapped Cole on the back carefully to avoid hurting his still-healing shoulder. "You'll do great. I was just messing with you."

"I know." Cole tugged on his tie again. "I hate public speaking."

He'd much rather be interviewing a suspect. That wouldn't be happening for a while since he was on medical leave. The only good thing about being shot was knowing Bryce, Susan, and her husband Mitch would never see the outside of a prison cell. All of them had taken a plea bargain. Life in prison in exchange for testifying against Justin.

Justin had refused to plead guilty to the multiple charges against him. But there was no doubt he'd been the ringleader. He'd drummed up Bryce's interest in Olivia by showing photographs of her to the twisted criminal. Then threw in payment if Bryce agreed to kill her. When Bryce got out of prison, he'd enlisted his cousin's help. Susan and Mitch were in so much financial trouble, they'd agreed.

The stalking was Bryce's way of terrorizing Olivia

242

before he killed her. It was something he was good at. Video footage taken from Oak Gardens proved Bryce had been there frequently while wearing disguises. He'd also shown up outside of Olivia's store and house. His disguises were professional grade and enough to prevent anyone from recognizing him.

In the end, Justin would go on trial, starting with Aaron's murder. Eli had reopened the case and uncovered evidence that proved Olivia's suspicions were right. Justin had bought bees online and placed them in Aaron's shed to kill him. Probably to get an inheritance when his brother died. Unknown to him, Aaron had already poured his life savings into Olivia's business. After that case was concluded, Justin would be tried for his involvement in the murder attempts against Olivia. A drawn-out trial wasn't ideal, but it ensured her safety, and in the end, that was the most important thing.

Justice would be served, even if it took time.

Olivia handed him some papers, bringing Cole out of his thoughts. "Here's a copy of your speech. If you get really nervous, focus on Eli and Sienna. They're the ones the toast is actually for. Or, if that doesn't work, look for me. I'll be in the back of the room, near the dessert table."

"Eli and Sienna. Or you. Got it." He swallowed hard as the DJ announced his name.

Olivia kissed him. It was fleeting, but sweet. "You've got this." Then she handed him a flute of sparkling cider to use for the toast.

Cole was bolstered by the confidence in her expression. He stepped onto the stage and took a deep breath.

Hundreds of eyes locked on him. The anxiety roiling through his stomach threatened to kick into high gear as adrenaline coursed through him. He did as Olivia suggested and focused on Eli and Sienna.

The couple was seated at the head table. Eli's suit was dark blue. He'd removed his cowboy hat, but still looked every inch of a country gentleman. He sat as close as possible to his beautiful bride, looking happier than Cole had ever seen him. Sienna was positively radiant. Her gown sparkled with thousands of beads, but it was the broad smile on her face that truly lit up the room, reflecting the joy and happiness in her heart.

Cole cleared his throat and introduced himself. There were many people in the room who didn't know him, since Eli and Sienna had friends and family in attendance that lived out of state. He also explained how he knew Eli and how long they'd worked together.

Then he took a deep breath. "As many of you already know, Elijah and Sienna were engaged once before, but difficult times drove them apart. It took an arrest and a murder investigation to bring them back together. Why? Because they're stubborn individuals who refused to admit they still loved each other."

Elijah and Sienna both laughed, as did many of the guests. Cole waited until there was quiet again. "Admittedly, I had my doubts in the beginning about your relationship. Above all, being a good friend means protecting those you love from being hurt. Elijah ignored all my warnings. Wisely so." Cole locked eyes with Sienna. "I'm not too proud to say I was mistaken about Sienna.

She is strong and courageous and absolutely perfect for Elijah."

Tears shimmered in Sienna's eyes and her chin trembled. Elijah hugged her closer, sending Cole an appreciative glance for his public apology. A private one had been given long ago, and Cole had already been forgiven, but this seemed the right place to affirm that he'd been wrong.

"Your romance serves as a reminder that the best love stories are not perfect," Cole continued. "Elijah and Sienna, you fought for your love. You embodied forgiveness and dedication. Loyalty to each other. You have helped each other through tough times and came out stronger for it."

Out of the corner of Cole's eye, he spotted Olivia swiping away a tear. She met his gaze, love shining from every ounce of her being. The feelings between them grew stronger with every heartbeat. They'd spent hours talking. Watched movies together. Spent time with Nana and Olivia's grandparents, as well as helping to put the finishing touches on Eli and Sienna's wedding. They'd even gone to church together.

Olivia's laughter brightened his day. Her gentle smile and the way she kissed him lit up his heart. Her kindness, her compassion, and her giving nature cracked open the vault inside him, releasing all the secrets he'd held close about his past. There wasn't anything Cole couldn't share with her. She was his safe place.

For the first time, he understood why all of his fellow rangers wanted to get married. When you had your best friend, a person who made your life better, why wouldn't you want to spend forever with them? With Olivia, Cole had a future. One filled with happiness and love. Maybe even children, God willing.

He focused back on Sienna and Eli. They would go the distance. He could feel it. The love between them was obvious and was deep enough to last a lifetime.

"Let's raise our glasses to a couple who embodies the essence of true love." Cole stepped off the stage and drew closer to Elijah and Sienna, lifting his champagne flute. "May God bless you both and may your love be a guiding light for today, tomorrow, and forever. Cheers."

Everyone raised their glasses and gave a resounding cheer. Eli and Sienna clicked glasses with Cole and then kissed. Moments later, Olivia was at his side. Her eyes were bright with happiness. "Fantastic. You brought half the room to tears, including me."

"Well, in all fairness, you're a softie who cries at every wedding. I don't think that counts."

She wagged a finger at him. "I wear my heart on my sleeve."

"Yes, you do, and it's another reason why I love you so much." Cole snagged her around the waist and drew her closer. "Have I said how beautiful you look tonight?"

"Only about a dozen times." She gave him a warning glance before her gaze darted toward the guests. "We're in public. And I'm working."

She had a point. Cole glanced around and spotted a small alcove. He tugged Olivia inside and then brushed her mouth with his. Her lips were soft and his heart skipped several beats as she leaned closer. Everything faded away as Cole's entire world centered on the woman in his arms. He never wanted the kiss to end.

She pulled away with a smile on her face. "Enough now. I really have to go to work."

"Then I'll have to save the rest of my kisses for later."

Her smile widened. "I'm counting on it. In the meantime, I have to check on the cake and make sure the DJ has the right songs lined up."

Cole reluctantly released her. "A wedding is a lot of work. Are you sure you're going to want to plan ours when the time comes?"

"There's no wedding I'd like to plan more." She winked at him and waved her left hand, wriggling her fingers. "But first you have to propose."

He waited until she walked away to find the caterer and then whispered, "I'm working on it, sweetheart."

Cole had found the love of his life. He was taking Nana's advice and holding on tight. He would spend every day working to make Olivia happy, and knew she would do the same for him. Cole wasn't naïve. He knew life would bring challenges and heartaches, alongside the happiness, but, together, they could get through anything.

He believed in them.

ALSO BY LYNN SHANNON

Texas Ranger Heroes Series

Ranger Protection

Ranger Redemption

Ranger Courage

Ranger Faith

Ranger Honor

Ranger Justice

Ranger Integrity

Ranger Loyalty

Ranger Bravery

Triumph Over Adversity Series

Calculated Risk

Critical Error

Necessary Peril

Strategic Plan

Covert Mission

Tactical Force

Would you like to know when my next book is released? Or when my novels go on sale? It's easy. Subscribe to my newsletter at www.lynnshannon.com and all of the info will come straight to your inbox!

Reviews help readers find books. Please consider leaving a review at your favorite place of purchase or anywhere you discover new books. Thank you.

Printed in Great Britain
by Amazon